I0539276

FOR THE LOVE OF KATRINA BINGHAM

Anne Carter

A Paulie & Kate Novel
Book 2

Beacon Street Books

Contemporary Alternative Romance

FOR THE LOVE OF KATRINA BINGHAM

by Anne Carter

Copyright © 2013 by Pamela Ripling
Cover © Pamela Ripling
Edited by J.R. Turner

ISBN-13
978-0615716329

Published In the United States of America

September, 2013

Beacon Street Books
Santa Clarita, CA 91355-2026
http://www.beaconstreetbooks.com

For the Love of Katrina Bingham

"Why do you stare at me while I'm driving? It's not easy, you know, switching back left side, right side, left side, right side, it's enough to send a man right off his rails."

Kate sat in her seat, sipping the shake, still belted in. "Does it feel funny, to you? Us, being here, just like this..."

"Funny, ha-ha, or funny, weird?"

"Just...like a flash back in time. Like except for Bonny being bigger, this day could be last summer instead of now."

Paulie stared at the steering wheel for a moment. "Are you rewinding, Kate?"

"Don't you ever wish you could? Would you, Paul?"

"I think about that a lot. Sure."

"To where? To before we met? Would you change things if you could?"

He turned to face her. "I think, if you could actually rewind, you wouldn't be able to change things." He thought for a moment. "Yes. I would rewind to the day we met. So that I could live it all over again."

"Even as it was?"

He nodded. "Absolutely. But I guess if you're going to talk about things that can't happen anyway, you might as well say, yes, I would change things the second time. Maybe I would take a different road one day when I'm, say, seven. Maybe I'd miss a beating by my dad, or have a better teacher, or something else that would change my path. Maybe I wouldn't be gay

"I would definitely rearrange some things, obviously. Maybe Jon would be alive. Maybe my mum would be alive. I dunno. But it's like on that television program about the future, where people do make changes and then other bad things happen. Like instead of Jon, someone else would die. Instead of being, well, the way I am, maybe I'd be straight but have a voice like a turkey vulture. A *fat* turkey vulture. Who knows."

"A fat turkey vulture?" Kate giggled, then leaned halfway across the console toward him.

"What?"

She puckered her lips. Paulie sighed, obliged her with a kiss. And another. He was never one to turn down a snog session.

DEDICATION

It has been said that a friend is someone who knows all about you—and still loves you. This goes out to all those imperfect friends and lovers...

For those who love without conditions.

Chapter 1

February, 1995.

A day like any other day dawned. London's fickle, intermittent sun teased as people walked and rode bicycles on the street, school children learned about dinosaurs, and shopkeepers hawked their merchandise. At home, the space shuttle Discovery was on the move, and President Clinton attempted to bail out Mexico. Wall Street set a new record. But in London's Snaresbrook Court, the day was like no other.

Paulie Bingham had been acquitted of murder. Those in the courtroom, for the most part, reveled in joy; only the victim's survivors did not share in the elation. Paulie's relief was palpable, yet so was his angst. His freedom had come at an immeasurable cost to one he held dear. Dr. Alec Doyle only shrugged when Paulie gave him a look of abject remorse and regret.

"You didn't have to do that. I had it all under control—no one had to know about you. About *us*," Paulie explained, after his release from the defendant's dock. "Your secret was entirely safe."

Alec, his blue eyes shadowed with fatigue, chuckled softly. "Under control? How so?" The doctor grasped Paulie's slender shoulder, not without obvious affection. "Don't worry, Paulie. It's done. It was right. I'd rather deal with the repercussions than see you put away."

Paulie hung his head. His ex-lover's words were exactly those he didn't want to hear. Alec's sacrifice—the exposition of his homosexuality—demanded a hefty price. While Paulie was glad, on one level, for the truth to be known, he didn't appreciate the circumstances under which that truth had surfaced. "I never meant for this to happen," he muttered.

"But it did, and we'll adjust. I think maybe it…it was meant to be. Now cheer up, dear. There's celebrating to do."

1

They did not return to Chanticleer that day, as the streets leading to Paulie's house were predictably, completely, impacted. Paulie's managers arranged for heavy security and a caravan of limousines to transport Paulie, Kate, Rob, Alec and Paulie's family members first to the Ritz Carlton, where they left the cars and rushed into the lobby, only to be escorted out the side exit and into a small, posh tour bus with blacked out windows, already half-filled with seniors awaiting a trip to Bath.

The bus delivered Paulie's entourage to The St. Martins Lane Hotel in the West End, where the 1000 sq. ft. penthouse suite, among others, was reserved for Stan Kowalski and Family. Before getting into the elevator, Kate perused the windows of the boutique shops just off the lobby. The window dresser was outfitting a mannequin with a simple burgundy party dress made of silk, with matching shoes.

"Can we come back later?" she asked, and Rob nodded.

"Whatever the lady pleases."

Rob and Kate had a suite of their own, one floor down from Paulie's rooms. Kate immediately phoned the U.S., sharing the extraordinary news with her parents and Cheryl. Rob stared down at the view of Covent Garden. "This is pretty awesome, even for me," he commented.

Kate came up behind him, slipped her arms around his waist. "What do you mean, even for you? You came from humble beginnings, like me."

"We've both stayed in some pretty nice digs over the past few years. This place is like 400 pounds a night. The penthouse must be a thousand."

"We all deserve it. Besides, record sales are through the roof. The verdict will sell even more."

"Is that what I should be doing? Getting arrested for murder?"

"Don't even joke about that! Your numbers aren't too shabby, either."

Kate went to the bar and opened the small refrigerator. "Do you think Paul will mind if I eat a granola bar? I can pay him back." She giggled. "I do have all his money, don't I?"

Before Rob could respond, the phone beside him rang. After a brief, apparently pleasurable conversation, he hung up.

"Was it Paul?"

"Yep. He wanted to talk to me, not you."

"I see. Best buddies, eh?"

"There's a party later, upstairs. He said I can bring a date."

"What do I have to do to get an invite?"

"Hmm. Maybe if you're good, I'll take you."

Kate slipped out of her shoes. "You know I'm good."

Rob pulled the drapes closed. "Wanna prove it?"

He met her halfway, took her into his arms. "I was thinking maybe we'd—"

Cut off by the doorbell, Rob sighed, left her to answer. He returned with a large, cello-wrapped gift basket, pulled off the card and handed it to Kate.

"Wow. How cool. Let's see..." She opened the formal, full-sized card bearing the words "in gratitude" on the front.

"Dear Kate and Rob, Just a little something to share in our joy. We could not have done it without your unflinching faith and love. I've never had the pleasure of serving such a devoted group of supportive friends. Times like these make the hard times, the losses, easier to deal with. Would that all goes splendidly from here onward. Cheers! Your most humble servants, William and Keith Teasdale. Who's Keith?"

"Kip. His son."

"Kip's his son? I had no idea."

"Not only his son. His *gay* son."

Kate's mouth dropped. "Now I didn't see that coming in a million years."

"And you. The expert on gaiety." Rob started digging into the basket. "Wow."

"I'm no expert. I didn't even know Brent was gay."

Rob stopped, looked up. "Brent was gay? Am I the minority in your life?"

She gave him a playful shove. "What's in the basket?"

"Candles...a bottle of Dom...chocolates...bath salts?"

"I see a theme here. Have you seen the Jacuzzi tub in there?"

"No, but I have a feeling I'm about to."

Kate raised her eyebrows. "You just stay right here. I'll call you when it's time."

The candles were scented, as was the Jacuzzi-safe bath salts. She lit the five candles, placed them around the tub. When the tub was full, she stripped out of her clothes, clipped up her hair, and settled into the hot water.

"Robbie! Get in here!"

He ambled into the room, leaned against the wall and stared at her.

"This is a picture I'll never forget," he murmured.

"There are more memories to be made *inside* the tub," she told him, beckoning with her eyes. He continued to lock his stare, slowly removing his clothes one piece at a time. Kate found herself salivating, craving his touch. She didn't have to wait long.

After a leisurely, relaxed couple of hours of sexual escapades, they napped on the exquisite king bed. Kate slept deeply, sated both by the lovemaking and the verdict. Rob woke her at 8 p.m.

"Kat girl. Wake up, princess. We need to go upstairs."

She stirred, moved closer so that her bare chest pressed against his. "Can't we be fashionably late?"

"Up to you. You want to piss off his lordship, be my guest."

She sighed, kissed his neck. "Okay." She sat up. "What time is it?"

"8:05."

"Damn it! The dress shop is closed now. I have nothing to wear to the party."

"There's that white bathrobe. Paulie wouldn't mind."

"I'm not wearing a stupid bathrobe to the party."

Rob got out of bed, went to the dressing room, then returned, carrying a garment on a hanger. "Okay. How about something like this?"

It was the dress from the store window.

"You—you bought this for me while I was sleeping?"

Rob smiled. "I had to guess at the size, which is extremely dangerous, so don't like slug me or anything."

She gave him a coy smile. "I'm sure it's fine. You sneak."

He'd picked up a shirt and casual jacket for himself as well. In the dressing room, she found matching pumps in her size. She slipped on the dress, thrilled with the fit, the sleeveless bodice and deep, plunging neckline. After fixing her makeup and hair, she emerged, gave a little spin.

"Too hot. Now I can't let you go up there."

"Oh, yes you will. I'm hungry; I could use a drink and a dance. And I want to see Paul and Alec."

"Well, I guess." He came close, touched her neck and drew his finger down to her throat. "Hmm. Definitely something missing." From his pocket he pulled out a small box, opened it himself and withdrew a diamond pendant. "Let's see how this goes with the dress and the cleavage." He fastened the delicate gold chain in place, centered the teardrop shaped stone against her skin. She was already wearing diamond stud earrings.

Kate turned to the mirror. "Oh, Rob. You shouldn't have. This is all too much."

"I have nothing else to spend my money on."

"It's gorgeous." She took a moment to thank him, kissing him greedily. "I'm afraid I have no gift for you."

"You are a gift."

A female bouncer met them at the door.

"And you are?"

"She's Mrs. Kowalski," Rob advised. "And I'm a friend of Stan's."

The woman looked skeptical. Kate sighed. "Katrina Bingham, and Rob Evans. Paulie will be terribly disappointed if you don't let us in. Actually, pissed off would be a better term."

A brief look of terror crossed over the woman's face. "Oh, Mrs. Bingham, I'm so sorry. I didn't realize...please, go right on in. Mr. Bingham is back there, near the bar."

"Thank you."

Paulie was, indeed, holding court at the bar. The suite was crowded, the mood upbeat and tinged with abandon. Alec assisted the rented bartender, and people danced in the small kitchenette that adjoined the living area.

While he didn't skip a beat of his intense conversation, Paulie did acknowledge her through the crowd. Rob kept a hand tucked around her waist as they made their way across the room.

Paulie handed her a pink martini, turned to Alec. "And Rob is a Chardonnay man."

"Right."

"Hello, darling. Rob. You've met Gray, my U.K. agent?"

Gray the Agent was in his late forties. He took Kate's hand, kissed it. "Ah, yes. The lovely you let get away. Shame on you, Paulie."

"Au contraire, Grayson. She was spirited away from me."

Gray turned to Rob. "Mr. Evans. We met in New York, two years ago. I just heard a cut from "No Doubt" a few days ago. Very good stuff. Will it be out soon?"

Rob smiled, took a glass of wine from Alec. "Thanks. Yeah, we're hoping for early summer. I'm the worst at meeting deadlines. It has to feel right. We haven't been very focused on anything over the past couple of months." Rob turned to Paulie. "But the world will start turning again any day now."

Clearly well into his cups, Paulie put his arm around Rob and kissed his forehead. Kate laughed and moved between them, gave Paulie a light shove.

"Hands off. He's mine."

Paulie grinned at her. "So you've got me sussed. Sorry, darling. Finish your drink. You need to catch up."

Behind her, Kate could hear Rob continuing to discuss music with Gray. She drank down her Cosmo and asked for another. It was a night for celebrating. They didn't have to be anywhere, drive anyplace, or put any children to bed. Paulie was happy and free, Rob was mellow and devoted.

Dance music blared from the suite's sound system, driving and exotic, charging the room with intense sexual energy. Kate moved up close to Alec, gave him a frown.

"What the hell are you wearing?" she asked, and, not waiting for a response, reached up to tug at his tie. "This is just wrong on so many levels."

"I told him," Paulie whispered loudly.

Kate succeeded in pulling the tie free and then wrapped it around Paulie's neck, tying it in a loose bow. "There. That's better."

Alec smiled, fussed at unbuttoning his collar. "Force of habit."

"Yeah, well, you have some new habits and vices to learn," Kate informed him. "Save that formal crap for the office."

"Didn't I tell you she was like that?" Paulie said to Alec. "Vixen."

Kate felt herself slipping into the mellow buzz of the martini. She turned back to Paulie. "Do you like my new dress?"

"I was thinking it's a damn good thing most of these guys are queer."

"Is that a compliment?"

He tilted his head, sighed although she couldn't hear it. He leaned close, whispered into her ear. "You are almost as much an attention whore as I am," he said.

Kate looked him up and down. He was wearing black leggings stuffed into knee-high bondage boots amassed with silver buckles, and a hip-length red and black zebra print swing coat with padded shoulders, over a black turtleneck. And Alec's red tie.

"Attention whore," Kate murmured, unable to keep the smile from her face. The music changed and Paulie's own "Love Specialist" came on, his most recent foray into a swaying blues accompanied by guitar and percussion. She saw it coming, couldn't step away as he tugged her close and rocked her in a slow, seductive little dance while he sang along with himself.

"I'm a love... love specialist...it's in my eyes...my eyes...the love..." And his eyes were closed, so she closed hers and tried to recall the feeling, the immense tidal wave of emotion that had almost drowned her when the verdict was read. Here was Paulie, her problematic, egocentric, mostly unstable soul mate, the father of her daughter; her confidant, one-time lover and sometimes brother. Free, happy, singing, loving, sexy, bi; still comfortable with taking her, pressing himself against her. No hesitation, despite the fact that both Alec and Rob were within touching distance. It clearly didn't matter to him.

A contented giddiness swept over Kate. They had such history that the feel of Paulie's body was a comfort, a known, a non-threat, she decided. No expectations, no fear, no commitments. Finally, perhaps, unconditional. A feeling that was almost taken away from her forever. Maybe that's how he felt, too. And there was more.

He couldn't sleep with her anymore, so he was screwing with her mind instead. Kate giggled with enlightenment.

The song dissolved into a dance re-mix of an old disco number, and Paulie released her but continued to dance on his own. She watched him, delighted, amused, and she took two steps backward, knowing she would back right into Rob's arms.

He wrapped her, slid his hands across the silky fabric around her waist.

"Don't be jealous," he whispered. "He's awfully cute, but I still like you best."

"That's a relief," she said over her shoulder, then, "Where did I put my drink?"

She was drinking too much. Too much to care, to pay attention to anything but having fun and abandoning everything else. So she didn't see what preceded Paulie's purposeful trek across the suite and into the bedroom with Alec trailing behind. The door slammed twice, and momentarily, Alec reemerged.

Kate looked for a place to stash her shoes. She and Rob had danced continually for the past hour, stopping only to refill their glasses and stuff hors d'oeuvres into their mouths. She looked up at Alec with a slushy smile.

"What's up, Romeo?"

"He's putting on the Bette."

"Bet?"

Alec took her shoes. "Bette. As in Midler. He's all worked up and pissy. Maybe you can talk to him. I surely can't."

"Nope. Not me. Not my job anymore."

Alec looked crestfallen. Rob turned Kate around to face him.

"Maybe you should."

"Why? He's not my problem now. Alec's just going to have to learn how to deal with 'im."

"We don't have a clue how bad the last two months have been for him. You are his best friend. Maybe you can help him to not melt down."

Chapter 2

The 'best friend' comment tugged at Kate. Rob was being awfully sympathetic. She thought for a moment, through the haze of the vodka, about Paulie's time in jail, the trial, the murder itself. The coming off of all that was bound to send him into a twist.

"Okay," she conceded. "I'll just check on him. Be right back."

She drank down the rest of her current drink, then wobbled into Paulie's bedroom.

"Paul?" she called softly. When he didn't respond, she went to the adjoining boudoir bathroom. He was sitting, staring at himself in the mirror. His hand was dipping into a jar of slap.

"What are you doing?" she asked in the same tone she would have used had she found Bonny with her hand in the peanut butter.

"Fixing."

"Fixing what?" Kate went to him, took the jar away. "Let me."

She dabbed the pancake makeup on his cheek, smearing it this way and that.

"Stop. You're making a mess." He pulled the jar away from her, upsetting her balance and causing her to fall awkwardly into his lap. She continued to touch his face. Now closer, she realized that his eyes were red-rimmed.

"You've been crying. What's wrong, Paulie?"

He shook his head, whipped a tissue from a box on the vanity counter and carefully wiped his eyes. "Go back to the party. I'll be okay."

"Did Alec upset you?"

"Is that what he said? Did he ask you to come in here?"

"Rob asked me."

"Rob? Why would he do that?"

"He said because I'm your best friend. He said you'd been through too much."

Paulie stared at her and his eyes began to fill again.

"Paul? Tell me, hon. What is it?" The room began to spin, and she squinted to focus.

"Did you see the photos?"

"What photos?"

He closed his eyes tightly, and tears spilled down his cheeks. "Of Jon," he whispered. "They made me look at them."

Kate put her arms around him. "Oh, baby. You don't mean...after..."

He nodded. "It was hideous."

"Why would they do that to you?"

"To get my reaction." He sniffed, and Kate held him close.

"I am so sorry, Paulie. How awful. How could they?"

He started to wipe his face, but she took over. She studied, dabbed, smoothed.

"You're right. I'm making a mess. I'm drunk."

"I know."

"Alec loves you, Paulie."

"He's not ready."

"Not ready for what?"

"Me."

Kate frowned, burped. "I'm sorry." She picked at his hair, and he brushed her hand away.

"Stop fussing. He's not ready to be out."

She returned her fingers to his head, rearranging the short, moussed spikes to her liking. He swatted at her again, and she fought him. "He—stop it!—He's spent his whole damn life hiding, Paul. You can't expect him to change in one day."

"Will you leave my fucking hair alone?"

He made her laugh, and she continued her assault. He grabbed her wrist and twisted her arm behind her.

"You are a little bitch. But you never had a problem being seen with me."

"I'm a woman."

"That's immensely clear, at the moment," he said, looking down at the way her dress had hiked up as she struggled to stay on his lap. "But still. You were being seen with a flaming queen. A skanky, baghead, cocksu—"

"Stop!" She slapped her free hand over his mouth. "Your voice is much too sweet, much too beautiful to be abused by such nasty words. And as for being seen with you, I was proud, Paul. It did me no harm. I know—" A hiccup interrupted. "Whew. Sorry. Um. I was saying, about Alec. He'll get better at it. Try...not to blame him. And let go of my goddam arm!"

"Where are your shoes?"

"I gave them to Alec."

"I kissed him. In the bar. He was embarrassed."

Kate sighed. He let go of her arm. "Are you fully aware of the sacrifice he made yesterday? For you?"

"He didn't want my going to prison on his conscience."

"Nonsense. He did it because he loves you. He lives and breathes for you. He'll make a wonderful partner if you let him. If you can be patient while he learns."

Paulie gave her a skeptical look. "I don't understand. If you love someone, you shouldn't have to learn."

Kate blinked, looked down, then back into Paulie's eyes. "I've learned."

He stared back, his eyes growing misty again. She touched his cheek, he turned away. The dizziness waved in and out, and she grasped his shoulder.

"You go back," he said softly

"Is there anything I can do?"

"You've done enough. More than enough."

"Are you sure? I can surly fix your face better. *Surely.* Fix it." She contorted, wiggled, maneuvered until she was straddling his lap, her bare legs wrapped around him on the bench. She twisted around, picked up one of his foam wedges and went to work on his makeup.

"I don't think I'm going to win this one," he muttered.

"Things will get better, darling. They will."

"Can you score me some skag?"

Kate paused, then stuffed the makeup wedge into his mouth. He spit it out in an angry fluster.

"Dammit, Kate!"

"You'd better not be wanting heroin, Paul. I kid you not, you go messing with that stuff again and I will disown you. I will disappear from your life, Bonny too. I won't be able to help you again."

"You twit. I was joking. That part of my life is long over."

Kate looked at his face, sighed. "You were right. I'm too pixed to fiss this mex."

"Then get the hell off of my lap before I forget, again, that I'm not straight."

She wiggled, pressed against him. And because she thought it would tickle him, she whispered in his ear. "You still make me feel hot."

"Then go take it out on Rob. I'm sure he'll be happy to oblige you. He's had a hard-on for you all night." Despite his words, his hand was on her thigh, sliding up beneath her dress to rest on her hip. "Is that my thong you're wearing?"

Had he asked her at that moment, she would have taken it off for him. Slowly, methodically, he pulled the hair away from her neck and pressed his lips just below her ear. A shiver passed through her, and her mouth filled with saliva. She groaned, swallowed, and was momentary immersed in the memories of sex with Paulie. Of obsession, need and dependence. She was wet, horny, confused, and sitting in the lap of the wrong man.

Kate took a deep breath, realized Paulie was watching her closely, reading her every thought. She straightened, pulled his hands away.

"What just happened there?"

He smiled. "You brought that on yourself, you know that."

"No, it was all your fault. Those damned silver buckles just turn me on." She edged back. "Will you fix things with Alec?"

He touched her bare flesh, ran a finger down her modest cleavage and lifted the diamond pendant. "This is some rock."

Kate nodded, felt what little power she had left ebbing.

"He means to keep you." He replaced the necklace, letting the back of his fingers caress. "That's good."

She didn't answer, didn't want to. Didn't want to go there, because it was a scenario she still held at bay. Inebriated, she couldn't trust her words, especially with Paulie. But he persisted, his eyes warm and, now, delving.

"Right?"

Her mood had swung again. She started to disengage herself, but he was quick to restrain.

"*Right*?"

Kate cleared her throat, lifted her chin, and shook back her hair. "Of course. Why wouldn't that be good? Now, I think I'm ready for a refill."

He released her and she stood up, tried to straighten her dress. An uncomfortable moment passed. She turned to go.

"We're not finished with that," Paulie said.

At the bedroom door, she turned back. "Yes, we are. Come back to the party when you're ready to be a grownup again."

"Slag off, Kate."

☞ *The girl never ceases to amaze me. We, as an erstwhile couple, never cease to be profoundly dysfunctional. I was more than certain that she and Rob had spent the afternoon fucking like bunnies; Alec and I had shagged on every available surface in our suite. And yet, here was Kate, and me, drooling to get at each other just hours later. I felt cheap- and yet, it all seemed perfectly natural. As much as I think I understand my dear little ex, she so often goes and changes the rules on me. Maybe that's part of the game, keeps it interesting. Did she really want to get into my pants? I feel for hetero men who have to learn how to suss it all out with girls. Men are quite obvious when aroused. But yeah, I do know Kate and she was ready to tumble. Was I?*

As time passes, my belief in a greater power is returning. I abandoned God when I was a rebellious, angry gay teen. But now, I feel His presence from time to time, and my wavering faith spills into my normally skeptical mind. It's because of Kate. I truly believe that she was sent to me for a reason, and maybe even, me to her. I no longer bother to count the times she's rescued me, booted my arse back onto the track when I derail.

Even unwittingly, like this night, when her mere presence forced me to push a freshly scored gram of Heroin into the bottom of my slap jar, then lie through my teeth to hide it.

Even drunk, which we both clearly were, she centered me. In that few moments we spent together, she quieted my grief about the photos, reminded me that Alec, too, is a gift. She pumped up my sexuality, fed that small, needy male part of me. She touched me with her thinly disguised vulnerability. She's not infallible, and that wee imperfection attracts me.

She also alerted me that something is not quite right between her and Rob. It was the only really negative thing about our little rendezvous, because a part of me was happy.

It's something I can't help.

Will we ever stop seducing each other?

I wonder how long before he found the hickey I left on her neck.

Flustered, Kate couldn't face Rob just yet. Didn't know if he would perceive her indiscretion, would know how close she'd come to joining Paulie in the sack. Kate was shaken, and as such, headed straight for the bar.

She wasn't a big drinker, and it didn't take much to knock her back. Even the sight of Alec pouring her next martini filled her with guilt. Did it show? Would Alec know how aroused she was, having shamelessly pressed her satin covered crotch against the bulge in Paulie's thin knit leggings? That Paulie had responded, and the mere memory of his fingers slipping between the thong and her hip was even now sending signals to her lustful mind?

"You okay?" he asked, handing over the glass. "Maybe you need to throttle back?"

"I'm fine. It's just warm in here."

"Did Paul upset you?"

"No." Kate took a sip, tried to focus. Of course he wanted to know if she'd calmed the boy down. "He's better. He's just recovering from it all. And," she took Alec's wrist, stood on tiptoe to whisper, "he's rather big on public affection, dear."

Alec colored. "I know I blew it. I'll get better in time."

"Yes, you will. Kissing is his second most favorite thing to do."

And I didn't kiss him before I left the room. It may have been a first. But then, whores weren't that big on kissing goodbye.

⚞ **I did sort of feel like a whore. After all I'd done or tried to do to separate that strongly physical part of our relationship, I'd gone and blown it. What was I thinking? Was it the alcohol? Was it the fact that I'd come so close to losing him completely?**

It certainly had nothing to do with just being horny. Rob and I had a very satisfying, fulfilling sexual relationship. The best I'd ever had. But that night, even as pickled as I was becoming, I was slammed with the realization that there was more to my obsession with Paulie than I'd known. Unhealthy? An understatement. Wrong? Clearly. Was it my fault, or his?

I never blamed Paulie for that stuff. I considered him too weak to control anything as strong as a physical attraction. I always took responsibility. Alec the Shrink, of course, chastised me for it. Even Rob accused me of letting Paul manipulate me. So maybe I wasn't in control as much as I thought I was.

I'd been climbing into Paulie's lap for almost twelve years. He'd been dipping his fingers into my undergarments for as long. Now, we were both on the verge of committing to other people. Was that it?

I spent the next hour sitting on a barstool next to Kip Teasdale, pretending to listen to his plans to follow in Paulie's pop star footsteps. Paulie came out of the bedroom just moments after I did, animated, smiling, greeting guests he hadn't spoken to yet. I'd managed to avoid Rob, as he was busy chatting up a busty blonde woman with big lips.

"Bloody hell," Kip said suddenly, and I turned to look across the room, to where Alec had Paulie in a full lip-lock. It was passionate, desperate, and overtly sexual. Of course I'd

seen men kissing before, many times. But never, not once, had I witnessed anything like this. Paulie had never been one of the men. A wave, something like revulsion, just washed over me.

It was my sober teen companion's quick reflexes that kept me from smacking my head on the bar when I fainted dead away. –Kate, the Queen of Regret

Chapter 3

In true rock star fashion, Kate kept the sunglasses on the entire next day. Every mirror returned the word "hangover" when she looked. The fog around her was denser than that London is usually known for. It was a fog of her own making, with faces coming in and out of focus. Rob, Paulie, Alec. Aspirin, coffee, eye drops. Luggage, passports, and goodbyes.

Everyone was subdued, and she didn't want to speculate on why. The trial was done, and Paulie was free to return to his life. Rob was his organized, capable self, making sure their flight to Albuquerque was on time. Alec seemed withdrawn and anxious.

Peg moped; the children all hugged Kate in succession. Kate couldn't wait to get into the limo, onto the plane and ultimately, into her own bed at home where she could sleep herself into a new life.

Only Paulie walked them to the waiting car. They ignored the remaining fans and paparazzi that still gathered on the sidewalk. The security guards Alec hired kept them at bay.

Kate looked down the street, toward the Heath, where Jon had met his killer. Remnants of morning mist clung to the shrubbery around Paulie's house. She was remotely aware of Rob shaking Paulie's hand, the driver loading their bags. She didn't want to say goodbye. Or anything else.

Paulie pulled off her dark glasses, fixed her with his eyes. Kate noticed his were bloodshot, too. He swallowed.

"I'm sorry," he said softly, sincerely. "You were right. It was my fault. Don't forgive me, or I will never learn."

Kate merely stared back at him, tried not to breathe. She wanted to point out the irony in his words, but couldn't open her mouth.

"Tell Bonny I will be home for her birthday." He bent down, kissed her temple.

She nodded once, then ducked into the limo.

Once on their way to Heathrow, Rob spoke up. "What was that all about?"

Kate shook her head. "Nothing."

"I'm going to guess it has to do with that love bite on your neck."

She felt herself color. Nausea welled. "He was drunk. Things got a little crazy. Nothing really happened."

"*He* was drunk. Uh huh."

"Okay, I was plastered. I felt sorry for him. *You* told me to go in there."

"I was drunk."

She turned slightly, to see his smirk.

"So drunk, in fact, that Alec had to carry you back to our room when you checked out at the bar. So Paul's not the only one who owes you an apology this morning."

Kate turned back to the window. "It's not your responsibility to take care of me. I passed out, for Christ's sake."

"A new side of Miss Katrina."

"A side you won't see again, hopefully."

"It wasn't so bad. I just wished I'd been the happy recipient of the hickey on *his* neck."

Kate sighed. "If he has one, he didn't get it from me."

"Must be interesting, having multiple lovers."

"I'm not his lover. Look, Rob, don't be mad at Paul. It wasn't only his fault."

"Aw, you're not going to forgive him, are you? Because he said—"

"He's a fool. We are all a pack of fools."

"Boy, when you're bitched out, you're really a pistol. Can we just call a truce?"

"Nothing to truce about. I'm not annoyed with you. This other thing will just go away."

"I'm not so sure that's going to happen. I think you two need to duke it out once and for all."

Kate removed her shades, looked Rob in the eyes. "Fighting isn't our problem. We need to just stay away from each other. We're toxic."

Rob considered, nodded. "If you say so. But Paul and I are friends. I can't help it if you two can't survive in the same air space without drama."

She put the glasses back on, turned back to the city sights rushing by. "Whatever."

It was possibly the longest day of Kate's life. Evelyn and Pop were waiting with Bonny at Albuquerque International, and after a brief hug and promises to call later, they boarded the last of three flights taking them back to Los Angeles. As usual, Rob had his car waiting at LAX, and fighting fatigue, drove them to Kate's house. It was only 6:30 p.m., but it felt like the 2:30 a.m. it was in Britain.

They sat in the living room for a while, answering Cheryl's questions about the trial. Kate's mood had leveled, but Rob's had diminished. Bonny was reluctant to leave her mother's lap. Despite her earlier malaise, Kate sipped on a glass of Merlot.

At 8:15, Rob stood. Cheryl kissed his cheek and whisked Bonny upstairs.

"You're not leaving?" Kate asked.

"Yep. Gotta go before I'm beyond driving ability."

"You should just stay here."

Rob looked down, hedged. "Naw. I don't...I don't really want to do that."

Kate shrugged. "I don't understand. But if that's your deal, well..."

"This was his house. With you. That room up there, that was your room with him. Feels...a little too...close for me."

"And Rachel never slept in your bed?"

Rob shook his head. "No. She was history by the time I bought the ranch." He drew a finger down her cheek. "Don't spaz out. It's just a thing with me."

Kate was stretched just thin enough that she felt her back rise up. "You can sleep on the couch."

"I'll talk to you tomorrow. You get a good night's sleep. Okay?"

"I'll miss you," Kate murmured.

"Not as much as I'll miss you."

She sat for a while, alone, after he left, let her mind wander over the events of the last few months. The important thing, she reminded herself, was that Paulie had beaten the murder rap.

Rob's discomfort with staying in her house annoyed her. What was the big deal? She was still pondering the thought when Cheryl returned, read her mind.

"Do we have bugs?" she asked.

"He's being an ass."

"Rob? An ass? How did his crown get so tarnished?"

"I didn't mean it. He's just got stupid rules."

"Things can't be too bad, you know you have a hickey the size of Texas on your neck."

Kate uttered a sarcastic chuckle. "Yeah. Except he didn't do that."

"No shit. Who did?"

Kate merely shook her head slowly, absently touching her neck.

"Holy fucking crap. You let Paulie suck on you? Are you *crazy*?"

"I was drunk."

"Drunk. Okay. Kate, you'd have to be comatose to get a note from home on this one. Did you sleep with him?"

"Hell, no."

"Surely Rob saw it?"

"He knows."

Cheryl poured herself a glass of wine. "You are bounding across thin ice, you know that?"

"Look Cher, the last thing I need right now is shit from you."

"Maybe you need a little more shit from somebody. I'm surprised Rob even bothered to give you a ride home. Jesus, even if you were drunk, how did you get into the position of letting Paulie fuck with you like that? Where was Rob while you were necking with Paul?"

Kate's face burned, for the umpteenth time. Despite her intoxicated state the night before, she remembered her wanton behavior quite well. A silent tear slid down her cheek.

Cheryl put down her glass. "Kate."

"I'm a freakin' mess, Cher. Please understand. They almost took him away from me, forever. I got him back. He was so disoriented, laughing, crying, joking, and suffering. I was doing what I do, you know. I was fixing him. I'd had about nineteen martinis. I was teasing him, that's all. Just, you know, playing around, like we always did. I didn't expect him to—to get turned on. He kissed my neck. I flipped back, back in time, back to those days when we shared everything and it was so erotic that I almost came, right there, sitting on his lap." Kate leaned her face into her hands. "And then, later, he was with Alec, and they were kissing, and...and...it just made me sick to my stomach."

"Kate, I swear. You have more shit in your life than Joan of Arc. You need to get straightened out, girlfriend."

"I know," Kate whined.

"First of all, don't, I repeat, DON'T sit on Paul's lap. First rule. Don't encourage pining ex-husbands who would still do anything to get into your panties."

"I know."

"Rule two. Don't go to parties with both new boy and ex boy in attendance."

"Okay."

"Get yourself a goddam chastity belt with only one key, and make up your mind about who should have that key.

"Four. If it bothers you to see Paul and Alec making out, then don't see them making out. Stay away, my dear girl. Damn. Here we were worried about Paulie letting you go, and you're still so fucked up about him. Let him go, for Christ's sake!"

"I just don't understand," Kate moaned. "How can he kiss me like that, and then be with Alec?"

Cheryl huffed, waved a hand in front of Kate's face. "Hello? Anybody home? Who's sleeping with Rob, then getting all cozy on top of Paul's package? Jesus H. Christ, Kat. You booted Paul for a reason. Get it together." She swigged the last of her wine, then trudged upstairs, leaving Kate to her sorrows.

She wept for a while, hurting because she knew Cheryl's every word was true. She was still crying when Bonny wandered in, dragging a tattered stuffed rabbit.

"Mummy?"

Unable to speak, Kate drew her daughter into her arms.

"Are you sad because Daddy didn't come home? I'm sad, too."

Kate embraced Bonny with desperation. Bonny patted her cheek.

"Let's go to bed, Mummy. I'll be with you. Don't worry."

With Bonny holding her hand, Kate retreated to her bedroom.

    ❧ *After Kate left, I rushed to see Dr. Ed, my London medical guru, who was sympathetic to my situation and prescribed Valium. It might as well have been baby aspirin. Of course, I doubled the recipe. My old mate Taylor brought me a ton of weed, and on these I survived the first few days of my new freedom. Alec frowned, but was otherwise loving and supportive. I've no idea how he's keeping his practice going in L.A., I'm afraid to ask.*

For a couple of days, I mourned the loss of the H. Now I realise how stupid that would have been. I can't risk losing the only people who truly love me. And my hard-won health.

Rob called me once to say Kate was cocooned in her house and he wondered if I was coming back anytime soon. I told him I didn't know anything yet, except that I'd committed to being home for Bon's 4th birthday. He wasn't himself and I'm sure I'm to blame.

She hasn't called me, of course. Didn't expect her to. We are both so crippled we have no business dealing with each other or anyone else, for that matter.

Teasdale called me. Apparently, the Yard is back on the sniff, looking for Jon's murderer. He wanted to know if I thought Ian Flynn could do murder. At first I said no, absolutely not, but as I think about it, he's a strange person with lots of unsettled anger. Yet he doesn't have the resources or the guile to have gathered all the personal info on Kate and the miscarriage. He couldn't have known about the trip to New Mexico. I never told him that crap.

Alec is thinking of relocating to London. I'm not sure about that, yet. I rather fancy my home here, in London, but I miss L.A. He says there is no reason we can't travel back and forth at will. Maybe --

My latest album, which had been sort of slunking around at the bottom of the charts, went double platinum this week. I am virtually back on top. Except that Kate has all my money.

I don't know what Kate's thinking. She was so blown out when she left here. It's probably better for both of us if we stay away from each other. Bonny's birthday is March 15th and I promised I'd be there. We can't let our ridiculous problems get in the way.

I'm not sure how it will be now, seeing her.

March 15, 1995. Calabasas, CA

Alec drove as they headed to Rob's ranch for Bonny's birthday party. Paulie leaned back, his eyes closed. The Valium was taking too long to kick in.

"You know what today is, don't you?" he asked.

"No, other than Bonny's birthday."

"Beware the Ides of March, my good man. It was today that Julius Caesar was assassinated."

"Bonny is hardly a Shakespearian character."

"True, but I'm a literal tragedy."

Alec chuckled. "That you are, my love. Don't worry. It will all be fine."

"Kate hates me. Rob likely wishes I'd been convicted. Bonny has probably forgotten me."

"There's always me."

"True. I haven't insulted you lately, have I?"

"Uh, let's see. Does throwing that hairbrush at me count?"

Paulie sank down in the seat, blew out a breath.

Kate had invited three little girls from the preschool Bonny had attended for a short time. Rob kept ranch staff busy with grilling and serving up the party fare, and leading the children around on the back of his old pony. Paulie met the parents, then had a joyful reunion with his daughter. Bonny refused to be put down.

"Don't ever go away again," she begged. "Let's go see Mummy!"

Paulie sighed and carried Bonny across the patio to where Kate sat chatting with Cheryl.

"Ladies?"

Cheryl stood up, gave him a brief hug. "Hey Paul. Good to see your unincarcerated ass-ets."

Bonny pressed her small hand to Paulie's cheek. "Kiss Mummy. She missed you bad and cried."

Paulie wished he'd taken something stronger. Kate didn't get up, so he leaned down, awkwardly trying to hang onto Bonny and kiss Kate's forehead. And do it quickly so that he could escape. "Hello, darling."

"Paul."

Alec rescued him. "Kate. Lovely, as usual." He took her hand, kissed it. "And Cheryl. I'm glad to see you on better terms."

Kate smiled at Alec, but Paulie saw it as polite and cursory. Empty, perhaps. He was able to hand Bonny off to her long-lost Uncle Alec and went to seek out Rob.

They crossed paths in the kitchen, where Rob was programming music for the outdoor speakers.

"Paul, man, I didn't see you come in."

Paulie forced a smile, but his anxiety was nearly unbearable.

"How's things?"

Rob shrugged. "She's—what's a good word? Troubled? Ever since you did the Lestat thing."

"Lestat?"

"You know, Tom Cruise, *Interview with the Vampire?* Ann Rice?"

Paulie shook his head, walked away to admire a painting on the wall. "It was a stupid mistake that I'll never live down." He shoved his hands into the pockets of his draw-string pants. "We were so loaded. She was playing cutesy, and I just, well, I barely remember even doing it. It wasn't anything, you know, real." *Barely, not.* He'd relived the whole incident a hundred times.

Rob was watching him, and took a deep breath, exhaled. "Okay. I get that."

"She was just trying to cheer me up. I was a train wreck that night."

"Understandable."

"So...you're not pissed with me too, are you?"

"'Course not." Rob returned to the music control panel, closed it up. "But Paul, I need to ask you something. If you think you're not done with Kate, just tell me."

Paulie forced a smile. Rob reached out to him, squeezed his shoulder. "I'll give you a good head start before I come after you, I promise."

"Decent man."

❖ *Cheryl's thoughts: It wasn't as bad as I thought it would be. Kate neither tried to seduce him nor scratch his eyes out, so I felt that was progress. Thank God for Bonny's sweet ignorance. She saved them.*

Rob surprised me, how he is just biding his time while Kate gets her shit together. Can't think he'll wait forever, tho. Kate is playing with fire here. I've stopped trying to tell her to get over it.

I met a guy this week I think is interesting. I met him at the gym. He's just finished a program and looks pretty hot to me, although he is older and has a shaved head, he's still cool. He seems interested so we'll see what happens. He's Canadian and I'm going to shoot him. With my Nikon, that is.

I know I shouldn't be so critical of my cousin. She's really suffering inside, and I can't help her because I think she's being asinine.

Paul is staying with Doc Doyle. No word on what his plans are, and I'm sure that got Kate's panties in a twist, too. I think Rob should take her and Bonny away for a while. Just my humble opinion.

Paul was high on something. Probably scared shitless of Kate.

Poor screwball Paul. —Cheryl

Chapter 4

May, 1995. Hollywood, CA

When Kate started preproduction work on *Independence Day,* she took Bonny with her. The film, about a massive alien attack on Earth, was right up her alley; she specialized in sci-fi, aliens and all things space age. Meetings, sketches, storyboards were a good distraction.

The past two months had been an unfolding. A time to recover from the difficult times, the missteps. She needed to center and get clarity, and still be able to hold her head up. The new job was a boost, and the re-connection with professional colleagues restored her identity. Part of it, at least.

Rob, as always, was her second. She and Bonny stayed many weekends at the ranch. They never spoke of the time spent in London; instead, they enjoyed being together and exploring their mutual interests. In mid-May, Rob committed to a concert for AIDS awareness in Santa Barbara. Kate weighed her options and decided to leave Bonny with Cheryl.

Kate's front row seat in the theater intrigued her; the wings were her usual vantage points. On stage, Rob fairly crackled with electric energy. His style of singing was urgent, emotional, and almost painful at times. Just like he did when they had passionate discussions, Rob gestured with his hands while singing, alternately patting his own chest and extending his fingers outward toward some unseen object. The spotlight glinted off of his silver bracelet and neck chain. Kate marveled as he switched seamlessly between guitar and piano, from ballad to driving rock. It was the first time she'd seen Rob perform since the only time, in London. *Paulie would be amazed.*

After Rob's set, the man sitting next to Kate got up and left, and soon Rob took his place.

"I guess the guy who was sitting here only came to see you," she whispered.

"He came to sit next to you."

Kate frowned. "A bodyguard?"

"A seat holder."

He took her hand, kissed the back of it. They watched the remaining act until just before the end, when they were quietly ushered from their seats and backstage.

"Babe, this is Don, Les, Nick and Frankie. Guys, Kate."

Kate shook hands with each of Rob's band mates. There was, of course, a party being talked about, and Kate wasn't surprised. She went along for the ride.

The pile of marijuana cigarettes on the coffee table did surprise her, however. She and Rob sat with the others on the glassed-in deck of Nick's beachfront home. Rob was first to light up, handing the joint to her next.

Kate stared, at first, then tentatively inhaled. She tried not to cough; it had been years. She handed the stubby cigarette back to Rob, the others having lit their own. The effect was almost immediate.

"Wow," she murmured, looking around the room through new eyes. Rob held the joint back out to her, and she took it, this time inhaling deeply and holding it in. He smiled at her.

Why was he smiling? Kate gave him back the cigarette, exhaled. "What?"

"Nothing."

Kate helped him finish the roach, then sat back into the couch, listening to the conversations around her and feeling conspicuous. Rob chatted with his friends, but Kate found it hard to follow his words. Something about Santa Barbara. The pier. The taxes. Or did he say Texas?

When was the last time she'd smoked pot? Visions floated past her, scenes she'd long forgotten. She was sitting on the floor, somewhere, leaning back against something, a wall perhaps. Paulie was lying down, his head in her lap. His hair was long. He wore his favorite Vivienne Westwood jacket, chattering on and on about Margaret Thatcher and something about being gay in Britain. He'd passed the cigarette to her, and she'd smoked the rest of it right away without giving it back. In retribution, he tickled her until she'd cried uncle, and they'd ended by having marathon sex on the floor. Kate smiled. It was, most likely, the night Bonny was conceived.

"Are you someplace good?"

Kate looked up. Rob was sitting beside her—but wasn't he sitting in the chair, before?

"I'm fine," she said. "I'm just...feeling mellow."

"Good."

Were they all looking at her? There were girls everywhere, it seemed. Girlfriends, wives, perhaps, yes, Nick was married, or was it Frank? Some of them were making out. When they weren't staring at her.

She got up, wandered down the hall to the bathroom where she washed her hands and checked her face to make sure there wasn't a reason for them all to be staring. A pale stranger looked back from the mirror.

I look terrible. I look worn out. Why didn't Rob tell me? Cheryl? Somebody?

She wanted to go home. She started back down the hallway, hoping she was headed the right way, when words wafted back to her from the living room.

"I don't know. She's not ready." Rob's voice.

"Have you asked her?" A girl.

"In so many ways, yeah."

"Maybe you need to drop a little ultimatum." A guy, not Rob.

Kate pressed the wall with both hands, as if it would fall in on her momentarily.

"I wouldn't do that. I don't know. I thought she was the right girl. Or maybe I'm not the right guy." Rob again.

"She's not still hot for Bingham?" The guy again.

"I think he's cute." Dumb girl.

"The guy's a fag, Tonya." Hateful guy.

"Look. Another subject, okay? Got anymore weed?" Surprisingly, Rob.

Kate slid slowly down the wall, inching her way to the floor, where she sat, knees drawn up.

You couldn't hold a candle to my crazy fag, hateful asshole guy.

And Rob, I'm sorry. I need more time. She closed her eyes, but Rob appeared, squatted down and kissed her cheek. She opened her eyes to his.

"You okay, babe?"

Kate nodded, and he helped her up. Back on the couch, she curled against Rob and tried to figure out who in the room she would kill first.

It was after 3 a.m. when they reached the ranch. Still stoned, Kate moved through a haze of warm and cold, good and bad, light and dark. Rob undressed her, tested her waters, and she responded. Under the influence of the drug, Kate felt different. Sex was different. She wasn't herself, she knew, but was powerless to be any other way. Driven by the images and thoughts of the night, and of the time she'd lived through since the separation, Kate dominated and bullied Rob, pushed him, shocked him. Soon, he began to dish it back, which only fueled her erotic attack. Love played no part in their mating.

At 5 o'clock, she dressed and found her bag. Rob didn't get out of bed.

"Okay to drive?"

"Yes."

He sat up. "Are you pissed off?"

"No."

"You didn't know I did pot."

"No. I didn't."

"Matter?"

Kate shrugged, transferred her bag to her shoulder. "I haven't smoked since before Bonny was born. I gave it up. I thought it would be irresponsible of me as a parent. She might need me, I might be in space."

"I get it. I'd never do it—I've never done it around her. You know that."

"Sure." She stared at him for a moment, hoping her head was actually clear enough to get home. "I need to go."

"Okay. Call me later?"

Kate nodded, sighed. She walked around the bed, leaned down, put her arms around him. "I'm sorry. I'm really sorry. You are the right guy, but I'm not sure I'm the right girl."

She rushed out then, before he could reply.

☞ *From Rob: How do you tell someone you love that she's in deep trouble? I'd been feeling things weren't right since we returned from London. Her happy times were missing the mark. Her sad times were dark and private, and she kept me at arm's length. I was about as tolerant as I could be, which is farther than most guys would go. As much as her relationship with Paul had never made sense to me, I accepted it. There were plenty of pundits around when I was married to Rachel, people who never saw what I saw in her.*

With Kate, it was always, "Love me, love my ex" and I just accepted that, especially since I truly liked Paul. I didn't think he was pulling her strings anymore, either. He seemed to be settling in with his new significant other, Dr. Doyle. So where was all this coming from?

I know Kate cares. But that night, she bruised me, inside and out. It wasn't lovemaking by any stretch of the imagination. It was brutal sex, she was anxious and angry and destructive. Funny, to someone who doesn't know her—she is so petite and sweet, taking on a guy like me. She wanted rough, so she got it.

I hated that she heard us talking. Especially since she was impaired and how do I know how that all sounded to her? I want her, badly. I want her to move in here, so I can wake up with her every day and be her protector and give her all the love, the good kind, the healthy kind, that she so needs and deserves. She seems like she wants it, but she's chained.

Maybe it is Paul she's chained to. If so, I feel like giving up. I'm no match for that kind of trial.

Still, I think she needs help. But I don't know how to give it.

July 7, 1995.

She would grow old and die in her car before the light at Melrose and LaBrea changed. Kate closed her eyes, tried to rub the headache from her temples. In the backseat, Bonny sang about the wheels on the bus, oblivious to her mother's tension.

New York. She'd known from the start that *Independence Day* would be shot there, but had purposely put the issue on the back burner. Front burners were still blazing. Now, she could no longer ignore the fact that production was ramping up on the East Coast, and she was expected to be there in two weeks if she wanted to work on the film.

"Mummy! The man's honking!"

Startled, Kate lurched the car into the intersection and turned on the green light, heading north. She was already late, and had promised to pick up some Thai food on the way home. Rob would already be waiting.

"Mummy, I'm hot!"

"Okay, Bon. Just...be patient. The car's been sitting in the sun all day. It'll cool off."

"Put the top down!"

"No, sweetie. Not today."

I belong in one of those Calgon commercials. Get me the hell outta here.

Traffic crawled up La Brea.

"I should have taken Highland. This is nuts."

"This is nuts!"

"And still much better than New York," Kate mumbled. She glanced in the mirror, tried to picture hauling Bonny around in a taxi. Ugh. She'd been to New York, once, on tour. Paulie was fascinated by Broadway, the Empire State Building and, of course, Times Square. All things that glittered, that excited. And while she didn't share his love of New York, she adored watching his delight.

Already tired, Kate struggled to lean into the backseat to retrieve Bonny. Her three inch heels didn't help, and she nearly twisted her ankle. She glanced nervously around; the Thai place was in a corner strip center next to a minimart and a bail bondsman.

"Uh, pad Thai noodles, tom yum, steamed green beans...and the yellow chicken curry."

"You want jasmine rice?"

"Okay. Yeah. Rice. Give me three servings of everything."

Bonny clapped her hands. "Yum! Rice!"

Kate dug into her wallet for a credit card, pulled one out and handed it. The proprietor looked at the card in question.

"You are Paul Bing-ham?"

"Oh! No, sorry. He's my husband. Sorry." She reopened her wallet, selected another card. "Here. This is the right one."

She took back Paulie's card and stared at it. How long had it been in her purse? She quickly pushed it into the slot behind her driver's license. "Sorry," she muttered again.

I just called Paul my husband. She shook her head, then turned at the sound of a hundred jelly beans pouring onto the concrete floor. "Bonny—", she began, but realized that the child vandalizing the gumball machine was not her daughter. "Bonny?" A fire alarm went off inside her head and she spun around again. "Bonny! Where are you?"

"Here, Mummy." Sitting in a chair not two feet away, quietly waiting, Bonny looked fearful. "I didnint go anywhere."

Kate's shoulders sagged in relief. "I'm sorry Bee, Mommy didn't see you there." She held Bonny's hand until the food was handed over the counter, wasted no time getting back into the car.

Rob was just drying his car when she drove up.

"I'm so sorry. Traffic was a frickin' nightmare," she huffed, carrying in the food with Bonny in tow. "Did you wash your own car?"

"Nervous energy. They always do a crappy job, anyway."

"Well come on in. Food's almost still hot. Cheryl inside?"

"Yup."

Although she was sure it was delicious, Kate barely tasted the spicy curry on her plate.

"When would you leave?" Cheryl asked. "You want wine?"

"Yeah. Please. Um, two weeks. They've rented out some big unsold apartment condo project. It's like weeks there, and then they're going to New Jersey, Utah, a bit back in California. It's a huge production."

"Do you want to go?" Rob asked, his eyes questioning even deeper than his voice. Kate picked up her wine glass, drank half of it down. Cheryl and Rob exchanged a glance.

"I do want to go. But I can't. And I saw that look. I'm tense, okay?"

Rob wet his lips, placed his hand on hers. "No look. Why do you think you can't go?"

"Because...I can't be away from all of you. I can't take Bonny there. It's an awful city. I'd be working twelve hour days, besides."

"Then just tell them."

Kate looked down. "It's hard. Hard to turn it down. Will Smith, Bill Pullman, Jeff Goldblum...they are all so nice, too."

"Something else good will come up. Something that shoots here." Rob said. "So stop stressing."

Kate finished her wine, picked up her fork. "Okay. Settled. I'm not going to New York. Pass the bottle, please?" she asked Cheryl, who handed her the wine. "And when are we ever going to meet your mysterious new squeeze? What's his name? Ralph?"

"Stan. You've been gone every time he's come over. He works a lot of evenings."

"What does he do?" Rob asked.

"He's a computer hack. He does work for the government. Intelligence stuff."

"Yeah, right. Does he work alongside Jack Ryan? CIA?" Kate jabbed.

"No, really. He does. He's also a musician, on the side. He plays at some jazz club in Hollywood."

"Well then. That's how we'll meet him, eh Rob? We'll just head down to Hollywood some night. It's not far." Kate decided.

"Great. I'd like that. But it's an over-21 place," Cheryl said, glancing at Bonny, who was stuffing green beans into her mouth with her fingers.

Kate pushed her plate away, brought her glass to her lips. "Well. I guess her father will just have to come back to take her for the night."

Cheryl smiled. "Sounds good to me. Hey Paulie, time to jump the pond and do some babysitting detail."

Rob frowned. "You're both joking, right? Is there no other possible babysitter than Paul? C'mon."

"Yes. We were joking. Lighten up." Kate picked up the empty bottle of Chardonnay. "Oops! There's more in the bar fridge. Be right back. And if you talk about me, I'll know, and I will get even."

⥽ How could I tell Rob, or even Cheryl, that I was coming apart at the seams? To tell them that, I would have had to have some notion as to why, and I didn't. Every day became a challenge. Things that usually rolled off stuck like thistles, painful, annoying. Rob did everything he could to cheer me, would have lassoed the moon and pulled it down if he could. Cheryl still harbored her annoyance over my behavior with Paulie before leaving London.

Rob and I were less intimate. I'd left us both battered the night we'd smoked up Nick's living room, something else I knew nothing about. The pot had unleashed a she-devil with something to prove. I only wish I knew what it was, because it was eating me alive.

New York had sounded good in one respect: it was a change. It meant getting away from the demons that I lived with in Paulie's house. And if Paul's house was so bad, why didn't I want to move in with Rob?

Because every time I thought about packing up, moving to Rob's ranch, I practically broke out in a cold sweat. The notion of commitment paralyzed me. By committing to Rob, I would be letting go of my other self. I stubbornly held onto my house, my life with Cheryl and Bonny...and my connection to Paulie, whatever it was. Becoming Rob's partner would disrupt it all.

I never asked who put it there, but the morning after our cozy little family dinner-just after which I passed out on the couch-I found a business card in my pocket. *Jane Creach, MFT. Marriage and Family Therapist.* After five more nights of drinking myself to sleep, I called her.

Chapter 5

July 15, 1995. Encino, California

"There's no need to rush. I've blocked off the whole afternoon for you, Kate."

Kate fidgeted. "I really don't know where to start. I don't know how much you already know."

"Assume I know nothing, like I've never heard of Paulie Bingham. The beginning might be good. Tell me how you met him."

"It's a long story."

"As I said, we have hours."

Kate nodded, rubbed at the finger that used to wear Paulie's ring. "Okay. The Story of Paulie and Kate, by the late Katrina Newman Bingham."

"Why do you say late?"

"Because by the time I get to the end, I may be dead."

She told the story of how she'd finagled her way into the tour, met and seduced Paulie. How she'd suffered, leaving him the first time.

"So I was jobless, homeless because my home was on the bus, you know. I got my pay from Buzz and got on another bus going back to L.A. Pain made me brash, made me not care, so I walked onto the set at Paramount the next day, after sleeping in the bus station. I fell in with a crowd of children taking a tour, so they wouldn't notice. I lied, just the way I'd lied to Buzz, and I somehow got a job there. Every couple of weeks I came up with new lies, and new jobs, until I was in the costuming and makeup department."

"That went well. You worked your way up."

"I kind of forgot about Paulie for a while. I pushed the thoughts away, because he was off being a big star. He had someone locate me once, so he could call me. We talked a few times, then just lost touch. Then I found out he was completely messed up on heroin."

Dr. Creach was quick to hand her a tissue.

"He was so lost. So sick. I was scared to death he was going to die in my arms that first night. He couldn't stop throwing up. I didn't know what to do, I was afraid to take him in to emergency. The press was already so bad. Had he not improved a bit the next day, I was going to do it."

"But he did improve."

"Yes. Somehow. And I took him back to L.A. and I took care of him."

Kate described the months she and Paulie had shared her small Hollywood apartment.

"Did you have sex?"

Kate blew her nose. "Yes. A few times. But I still knew he was gay, and sometimes when we were out he would elbow me and say, 'ooh, look at him. I'll bet he's good.' And it hurt. So I took him out one day and bought him a house and moved him."

"That must have been difficult."

"I thought it was at the time."

"And then you separated yourself, again?"

"Yeah. That's when I met Ray Goff."

It took the better part of the afternoon for Kate to tell the rest of her sad tale to the therapist. She felt better having told someone, about her secret desires, her fears, her joys. Because although Rob knew some of it, Cheryl knew most of it, even her mother had heard parts, no one knew it all, how the parts fit together, or just how badly she'd damaged herself in the process. At least Kate considered it damage.

"Let me ask you a little about your family. You mentioned clashing with your mother."

Kate looked to her lap. "My mother. Mom can be outspoken at times. Plus, I was kind of a rebel when I was younger."

"If you could describe each of your parents in a few words, how would you do that?"

"She's strong, can be controlling, but a caregiver. She works hard, takes care of everything. My dad, well, he's quiet.

People like him, he's always calm. He's very smart. He's the one I always went to when I wanted something."

"What does your father do for a living?"

"He designs airline interiors."

"Your mom?"

"She used to be a hospital administrator. She's retired now."

"Do you ever see yourself as…similar to your mother?"

Kate twisted her face into a surprised grimace. "Are you kidding? I'm nothing like her."

The therapist nodded, reviewed her notes. "Let's switch gears. You said that seeing Paulie with his new lover hurt you. Did you engage in kissing Rob in front of Paulie?"

"I guess so. Sure, I must have."

"And how do you think Paulie felt about that?"

Kate averted her eyes. "I don't know."

"Don't know, or don't want to think about?"

"That's part of the problem. I don't know how Paulie feels now about anything. I used to be able to read him instantly. We shared every thought. He cried like a baby when I made him leave. But as I said, I just couldn't face sharing him or making him miserable any longer. We both cried. We made love. He moved out the next day. Since then, our communication has been all screwed up.

"We're not honest anymore. Sometimes I think he's doing it for me, you know, so that I can move on. Then I think, maybe he's really okay with it. Things started to get better, at one point. Rob and I began to connect. Then the murder trial thing happened, and everything just blew around like leaves in a whirlwind. I got to Paul as quickly as I could. We were together again, if only briefly. When it settled, we were both shaken. That's when the lap thing happened."

Dr. Creach smiled, put down her pen. "You are really fixated on that incident."

"Well, hell, yeah! I was the one who pushed him away. He would have stayed married to me, probably forever. He loves me." The tears poured down Kate's cheeks. "And I pushed him away. He didn't know what was best for him."

"But you did."

"Of course I did. I always do."

"And because you pushed him away, you were not allowed to invite him back by sitting on his lap and encouraging sexual advances."

"No. I most certainly wasn't allowed to do that."

"But you acknowledge that you were intoxicated. That he was also intoxicated."

"No excuse. I knew better."

"Better, how?"

"I knew how he affected me. How we affect each other. It's an addiction."

The therapist nodded, made a note. "When was the last time you saw your ex?"

"March 15th. He and Alec came to the ranch for Bonny's birthday party. They stayed in town for a few days and then went back to London."

"Did you talk to him then?"

"No. Not at all."

"So. Four months have passed, and you haven't spoken with him."

"No. Well, yes. He calls every week to talk to Bonny. So I answer the phone, but we don't really talk. It's how-are-you, all's-well-here, that kind of crap."

"Let me ask you something, and this isn't a test, or something I'll write down. You won't have to answer for it later. What do you think you want? If it was a perfect world, and you could orchestrate things to your liking?"

Kate thought for a moment, still teary.

"It's okay. No one but me will ever know what you say. And I won't judge you, Kate."

"I can't tell you."

"Can't or won't?"

"Can't."

"Think of a time, then, when you were happy. When you were the most carefree, everything was looking up, and nothing could possibly go wrong. Can you recall such a time?"

Kate nodded immediately. "It was in Barcelona. I'd just found out I was pregnant again." She sniffed, smiled. "Paulie is really unreliable about condoms. I can't take the pill, so I started using a diaphragm. Then I left the damned thing in the hotel bathroom in Amsterdam, which is where the tour started. Anyway, somewhere after that, I got pregnant, and in Spain, I told Paulie. He was so happy, and the tour was going well, and Europe was so incredibly beautiful."

"This was just before all the bad stuff that happened in London."

"Yeah. We were immensely happy in Paris, in Bern...we toured Prague, and we took a day to explore Lisbon...so if I could go back, I would go back to those two weeks. I would...I would find a way to keep Paulie home from that stupid party. That one night changed everything. Jon would still be alive. And... and... Paulie and I would still be together."

Her sobs were heart-wrenching and uncontrollable. Dr. Creach came off the adjoining couch and cradled Kate in her arms.

"Okay. Okay. I understand."

Kate straightened, accepted fresh tissue. "Oh God. I am so sorry. I'm such a mess. I'm such a fool! Have you ever seen anyone as foolish as I am?"

Her new best friend grinned. "Well, possibly, yes." Dr. Creach returned to her place. "How do you feel now, having spilled it all out to me?"

"Better, and worse. How's that for an answer? It feels better telling it. It feels worse reliving it. I really see how bad off I am."

"You haven't shared much about your feelings for Rob. Can you explore that a little?"

Kate sagged. "Every cell of my rational mind says he's the perfect man for me."

"But your irrational mind is sabotaging you?"

"I don't know. He's just everything any girl could want."

"Are you any girl?"

Kate paused, tilted her head. "Apparently not. But if I let him get away, I know I'll be sorry. He's just so...wonderful. Bonny loves him, Mom and Pop love him. He's incredibly good to me, he tries to understand about Paulie. In London, he supported me without question. Supported Paulie. He didn't even get mad about the hickey. What kind of miracle is a guy like that?"

"Okay, we've established Rob Evans as God's gift to the single mother. Everybody loves this guy. But do you?"

Her patient was quiet, so Dr. Creach continued. "Do you ever think about your future, Kate? Do you think about things like, Bonny losing her first tooth, graduating middle school? Do you think about going to the Rose Parade on New Year's Day, or taking in a Dodger game on a lazy Saturday afternoon? How about Christmas morning? And when those scenes pass through your mind, as they surely must sometimes, do you see Rob Evans beside you?

"You mentioned something earlier about being pregnant. Have you thought about what it would be like if you became pregnant again, only with Rob as the father? These are the things I want to know."

Kate swallowed, unable to speak.

"You certainly don't have to answer these right now. But I want you to think about these questions. And I want you to think about them in the context of Paulie not being in the picture, if you can do that."

"But...what if...it's Paulie I see in those pictures?"

"Then that would be very telling."

Dr. Creach closed her tablet. "Kate, you dredged up a great deal of emotion today. Tonight, you will be especially vulnerable. I suggest you rent a movie, have some comfort food and spend the time with your daughter, who is the only true constant in your life right now. A lot of stuff will be churning around. Some of it good, some of it painful. Come back next week and we'll see where you're at."

"Should I avoid Rob?"

"Only if you want to. Just, tonight, don't put any demands on yourself, okay?"

She took the doctor's advice and got a couple of movies, one for Bonny and one for herself. She popped corn and the two of them sat in bed watching.

"This was Mommy's favorite movie when I was little," she told Bonny. "*Sleeping Beauty*. There's a scary old witch, but also a handsome prince."

"Like Daddy."

"Just like Daddy. Yeah. Sort of." Despite the irony, Kate smiled. Bonny barely made it to the end of the film, and then Kate put on *Somewhere in Time*.

Midway through the movie, melancholy seeped in and she turned it off. "That wasn't the smartest choice," she murmured, turning the television back to regular broadcast. Jay Leno was funny, and then gone. Old movies dominated the tube, and she watched *The Maltese Falcon*, and then, *Bye Bye Birdie*. She marveled at the talent of Paul Lynde, a closeted gay actor who portrayed the role of the father in the 1963 film. How different things were today, she thought, and naturally, her mind turned to Paulie.

Kate pointed the remote, turned off the tube. She edged over and snuggled with her sleeping daughter. Opening one eye, she peeked at the clock. 3 a.m.? Tomorrow would be a late morning. She'd already tendered her resignation to the production company, and was currently unemployed. It wasn't like she was hurting for money, however.

Unable to find comfort, she turned away from Bonny, stared at the other nightstand, the other clock radio. Paulie's side of the bed. Dr. Creach was right, it was like having some kind of virus. She felt off balance, disoriented in her own body. Unbidden thoughts rose and she mentally swatted them away. What was she thinking about? Oh, yes. The money.

Paulie's money. She'd gone to the bank yesterday, had fixed all the accounts. Had also asked her attorney to switch everything back. She'd forgotten to tell Paulie.

It was as good an excuse as any. She picked up the phone. It was four angst-filled rings before he picked up with a groan.

"This better be good."

"I'm sorry, I thought you'd be up." She kept her voice low so as not to wake Bonny.

"Kate? Darling! Wow. Um, sorry, I'm...hold on."

Kate could hear her heart beating in her head. Beating fast. *Obsessed girl fan calls rock star idol! Film at eleven.*

"There. So, what's up? Christ, it's like 3 a.m. there. What's the matter?"

"Nothing. Nothing's wrong. I just wanted to tell you that I gave you your money back. And it's quite a lot more than when you gave it to me, by the way."

"Brilliant. Do I owe you a commission?"

"You owe me something. Not sure what."

"I see. When you figure that out, you're welcome to come and collect."

Kate felt herself smiling. "Is...is Alec right there?"

"He was. He's a bear, far worse than me in the morning. So I moved away from that bit of nastiness. I'm now downstairs putting up a cup of tea."

"Ah. Up late last night?"

"Always. You haven't told me why you are up during the middle of the night. Trouble sleeping?"

"You sound worried."

"Perpetually."

Kate drew her knees up. Something in his voice, some minute inflection touched her deeply.

"I wanted to apologize," she said softly. "I was a hag when you came here in March."

"I was an arse when you left here in March."

"So we're both a couple of losers. I just didn't want to leave it that way." Kate held her breath for a moment, then plunged forward. "I miss you."

He was quiet, and Kate chastised herself. Dr. Creach had warned her. She should have kept her stupid mouth—

"I miss you, too. Enormously."

She exhaled. His few words were the first to lift her spirits in months.

"Talk to me, Kate. Bring me up to date."

"Well...I almost went to New York. The picture I'm working on, *was* working on, well, some of the production filming is back there, but I just couldn't make myself go. It's a lot, right now, and I wasn't in the right frame of mind, you know. But nobody, nobody could help me decide. Nobody really thinks like I do, they all just sit around and ask me what I want to do, and how should I know? They can't help. I had to decide it all alone, and it was a huge decision, you know, because of Bonny, and all. They don't get the thing about my career, either. This will hurt me."

"You should have called me."

"You?"

"Me. I know your mind. I also know exactly how you feel about New York, and about Bonny. I would have helped you decide, darling."

"But I'm...I'm not allowed to call you, Paulie."

"Says fucking who?"

"Because we're trying to learn to live apart, right?"

Kate waited for his response but only heard grumbling.

"How are things with you? Your turn to talk."

He was pacing in his kitchen, she could tell.

"Let's see. I got a tattoo last week."

"Where at?"

"This little shop in Clerkenwell."

"I meant, where on your body?"

"Kate, you would have laughed your trim little bum off. I go in there, and this bulldog biker type is reading some girlie magazine, and he looks me up and down. I say, 'I want a tattoo,' and he says, 'I don't do dicks.', so I say, 'Who you calling a dick, asshole?'"

"You didn't!"

"So he says, 'I wasn't calling you a dick, wanker. I was saying I won't ink your fuckin' dick.' So I say, 'While that makes me very sad, it's all right, because all I want is a wee littl' butterfly on my nipple, sweetheart.'"

Kate again stifled her laughter.

"I ended up at the shop next door where the tatt artist was a much nicer fellow."

"Did it hurt?"

"In a word—yes. I'd never do it again. Oh, did I tell you Alec wants us to stay here, now? He's thinking of setting up shop in Kensington."

"And you? What do you want?"

"Well I guess if we're supposed to be learning to live apart, I should bloody well stay on my side of the pond."

"Aside from that?"

"Give me one reason, however miniscule, to get on a plane and I'll be there."

Kate giggled, then covered her mouth when Bonny stirred.

"I'm serious, Kate. Our secret. Make something up. Tell me your attorney has ordered my physical presence to sign some stupid document. Tell me Bonny is demanding a paternity test because she can't believe someone as loopy as Paul Bingham is her father. Tell me you need a heart transplant and I'm the only match."

"Stop. You'll make me wake her," she hissed, trying hard not to rouse Bonny with her laughter.

"She's there, sleeping with you?"

"Yes."

"Not Rob."

"Rob doesn't sleep here, Paul."

"What do you mean 'doesn't'? Ever? Did you break up?"

"He won't sleep here. He never has. Because of us. Because this is our marriage bed."

"Whoa."

"Yeah, huh?"

"That's bizarre."

"He wants me to move in with him." It came out before she thought. As easy as if they were still together.

"What? Oh, hang on, just—good morning, dear. Tea's on, muffins are heating."

Kate strained to hear Alec's response but heard nothing.

"Now, what did you say? He wants you to move?"

"Yeah."

"So what's stopping you?"

"I...I don't want to."

"I find that very interesting."

"Actually, so do I. I guess I have commitment issues."

"Commitment issues. I rather fancy that term. Why do you suppose that is?"

Kate took a deep breath and released it slowly.

"It's better left discussed at another time, don't you think?"

"If you insist."

"It's just complicated."

"Everything is. Our birthdays are next week. What do you want? Or are you not allowed to tell me?"

"Not allowed. Definitely not allowed."

"I see how it is. Can I tell you my wish?"

"Will it mess me up?"

"Darling, we are both messed up beyond repair, I'm afraid."

"Well, all right then. What do you want for your birthday? Besides to be 21 again."

"I was 21 when I met you, Kate."

Kate considered his comment, asked the question she'd wanted to ask forever.

"Would you do it again? What we did?"

"In a heartbeat."

A comfortable quiet passed between them.

"You'd best get some sleep, my love. Kiss Bonny for me."

"But you haven't told me your wish yet."

"You know my wish." His sigh was audible. "And let me know when you are ready for that heart transplant."

New Patient: Katrina Newman Bingham. Age 34. Divorced.

Complaints: Depression, lethargy, increasing dependence on alcohol; confusion, life issues;

Onset: Separation and subsequent divorce from husband, relationship of eleven years.

Note: Husband is both internationally famous British pop star and homosexual. (Bisexual?)

Family: Parents both living; no siblings; daughter, Bonny, with husband, Paul; close to maternal side cousin, Cheryl Collins, who also lives with the patient and is part-time caregiver for the child. Dating Robin Evans, another music entertainer.

Today was our first visit. I heard a most fascinating story of Kate's relationship with her ex-husband, Paulie Bingham. Patient is experiencing episodes of profound sadness and depression, and is having difficulties making decisions. She has some classic, post-divorce syndrome characteristics. However, her relationship and the reasons for the divorce are somewhat atypical. Special circumstances include the fact that Paul Bingham is a homosexual man. The two bonded as young adults, became dependent upon one another, but found their preferred lifestyles to be in conflict.

Despite my obvious policies about staying the course and keeping the distance, I found myself sympathizing with Kate more than once. She called the love they shared an addiction. She used the words "obsessive" and "co-dependent" more than once. She's extremely devoted to this man, and takes an almost defensive pose when questioned about his value or worth. She's as protective of him as a mother bear, and yet, describes their sexual relationship in healthful terms.

Kate also has issues about commitment to a new partner. While she finds Evans attractive, nurturing, strong, and containing all the qualities she feels she needs, she is unable to move forward with that relationship. It is clear that her feelings for her ex-husband stand in the way.

I suspect that Kate is more like her mother than she wants to acknowledge, and her need to control and nurture led her to Paul's need to be controlled and nurtured. His sexual orientation wasn't a strong enough deterrent to keep them apart. Because she hasn't experienced a conventional, stable heterosexual relationship, Kate has no reference by which to gauge her feelings. Evans' strength and masculinity confuse her.

By the end of the interview, I found myself wanting badly to also talk to Paul Bingham. Since he is abroad, I doubt this will occur. She is going through a very difficult time. I believe that she really does know exactly what she wants. But the conflict, in her case, is exceptional. I don't know if there is a win-win here. See case file notes.

M. Creach, July 15, 1995.

Note for next visit: Ask Kate if she called Paul after our meeting. A bet I have with myself.

Chapter 6

July 22, 1995. Chart House Restaurant, Marina del Rey, CA

"Happy Birthday, Kat." Rob leaned close to kiss Kate. His cologne enchanted, and she grasped his jacket lapel while they kissed.

"Hey, hey, hey. Enough of that." Cheryl waved her hand at them across the table. "Get a room."

"We have a room reserved...later," Rob said. "At home."

Kate smiled. She felt good, had felt worlds better for the past week. Two visits with the shrink and one delightful phone conversation with Paulie. Things weren't fixed, not by a long-shot, but the world wasn't quite so grim and grey.

Especially tonight. They celebrated not only her birthday, but the anniversary of their first date—which had technically passed, but hadn't been acknowledged. Cheryl, too, had announced the opening of a gallery showing of her photographs in Pasadena. The only thing marring the evening was Stan's last minute cancellation.

"I don't understand. He was fine this morning."

"The flu comes on fast," Rob said. "I'm glad he didn't show up here, coughing on us all."

"We'll meet him another time, Cher. Let's plan a barbecue or something next month."

"Sure. That would be cool."

Rob pulled an envelope out of his inside breast pocket. "Here. Open this before the food comes."

Kate slipped her finger under the flap and opened the card. It was simple, heartfelt, and romantic. He'd signed, "Love, Rob."

"I'm better at songs than at sentiments. But the card says it pretty well."

She kissed him again, and he pulled out a second envelope. "This goes with that."

"What?" Confused, Kate opened the second, longer envelope. "Plane tickets? Oh my God! And what's this picture of?"

"It's a little house, on a private beach, on Maui. Belongs to a friend of mine. He's never there, he's always on the road, so I thought, why not? Bonny will love playing in the sand."

"I don't know what to say. What a great idea. When will we go?"

"Up to you. All of August and most of September are open. We can stay a week, two weeks, whatever."

Cheryl beamed. Kate tilted her head. "Did you just swallow a canary or something?"

"Me? No way."

"Well," Rob began, giving Cheryl a sympathetic smile, "you did let it slip that Kat had never been to the islands. Left her footprints on the banks of the Seine, but never dipped her toes into the bathwater of Hawaii. I had to fix that."

The waiter placed their dishes. "For the lady, the parmesan-crusted Shrimp Fresca with angel hair pomodoro, and steamed asparagus."

"Robbie, could we call home?"

"She's fine, babe. The last time we called, Nick said she was already in bed sleeping."

"Just in case."

He complied, and Kate felt better. There was something discomforting about leaving her daughter with the pot smoking Nick Valente. But then, Bonny's own father had used every drug imaginable, and still rolled a spliff or two a week. Nick's wife was very nice, though, and Kate was fairly certain she was not the one who'd commented about Paulie.

After dinner, Cheryl tossed her a small wrapped gift, a silver charm bracelet with a single charm. Engraved on one side of the heart shape were the words, "Believe in you" and on the back, "Cher to Kate, 1995". Kate immediately put it on and hugged her cousin.

They shared a hot chocolate lava cake.

"So when do you think you'll go?" Cheryl asked, licking the thick, Godiva chocolate from her spoon. "When can I have the house to myself?"

"I need to check my calendar, you know, to see when's a good time."

"Don't wait too long." Rob gave her a brief, solemn look. "It will cool off before long."

"I'll bet he's gonna ask you," Cheryl said, as they stood together putting on lipstick in the ladies' room.

"Ask me what?"

"To tie the proverbial knot, blockhead. In Hawaii. I'll just bet that's his plan."

Kate froze, stared at Cheryl in the mirror. "Did he tell you that? C'mon, really?"

"No. He didn't. It's just a hunch."

"God, I hope not." Kate rolled down her lipstick and put the cap on. "That would be...bad."

"Bad? Really?"

"Cher, I can't even commit to moving in with him. Marriage? I can't think about that right now."

"Then maybe you should come clean and tell him, and quit leading the guy on."

"You think I'm leading him on?"

"Is there an echo in here? Shit. I'm sorry if I ruined your day."

"No. You didn't. Forget about it. Forget what I said. I'm just tired, and I'm uneasy about leaving Bonny." Kate started to go, then paused. "Look. Remember something, okay? I've been married before, and I just went through a very painful divorce. I'll be the first to admit I'm not quite over it. It was a magnitudinous failure, and I'm a little gun shy right now. Rob, he's been single for something like six years. He's very level headed, he knows what he wants. I don't blame him, but I'm just not there yet. Please cut me a little slack?"

Cheryl stared, then nodded. "You remember something, too, Cuz. I've never been married. I've never been asked. I've never experienced the kind of love you have from either Paulie or Rob. I'm 36 years old, I've been cheated on and had an abortion, and now I'm afraid every guy I date will turn out to be a clueless flake. So forgive me, too, if I seem a little dismayed by your choices. You know I love you." She gave Kate a brief hug. "And don't you dare open your mouth and say you're sorry."

∾ I felt like a royal ass that night in the restroom. I knew I'd been taking Cheryl for granted, for a long time. But she made it easy to do so. I never thought about her loneliness, never considered her to be hurting or fearful of growing old without someone to love her. She was so beautiful, so smart, so sassy-I was always jealous of her. She was blonde, for Christ's sake. She told people she was 5'9", although I knew she was really 5'10". We once jokingly wished we could average our heights. She was athletic, top of her class, and had a terrific, dry, sense of humor.

Maybe she was too perfect. Paulie once told me that girls like Cheryl intimate some guys. I always hated being short, but Paulie said it was an asset. Guys might look at tall girls with lust, but short girls were a lot more accessible. I asked him how he would know. He didn't date girls! In retrospect, he was just flirting around with me. At 6-1, he's over a foot taller than me: in bed, I climbed him like a tree.

Worse than Cheryl's confession, I had a new worry now. Cher was rarely wrong, and her prediction about Rob scared me back under my rock. I'd just seen Dr. Creach that afternoon, and now it would be another week before I could get in and spill my crap to her. I don't think Rob was talking about the weather when he said it will cool off soon.

The doctor asked me about the phone call with Paulie. She said she'd expected me to do it, and I was instantly filled with guilt. She reminded me that there was no penalty, then asked me to tell her what we talked about, so I did. I regretted repeating the part about Paulie begging me to concoct an excuse for him to come to Los Angeles, because as I recounted it, I was reminded of Rob's belief that Paulie manipulated me with words. I was deeply afraid that Dr. Creach would confirm Rob's suspicion. But she only made notes, and asked me why I thought I felt so much better after talking to him. I wasn't sure what to say. I told her I guessed it was because he

was still my best friend, and didn't people who were hurting usually feel better after talking with their best friend? I felt connected, for the first time in, what, oh my God, I said, it's been a whole year. More than a year since Paulie moved out of our house that heartbreaking day in June of last year.

The one thing I didn't say was that I felt Paulie's love across the phone lines, across the ocean, across the cosmic and unknown space between us.

The anxiety returned. Kate found reasons to keep her conversations with Rob short during the week that followed, as she waited for her session with Dr. Creach on Friday. Fortunately, final work on his album preoccupied Rob, who was apologetically scarce anyway.

By mid-week, she was poring over *Variety* for news of any films going into pre-production. If she could get a job right away, it might conflict with any trip to Hawaii before the fall. It was stupid, she eventually realized; if Rob was going to propose, he wouldn't need to be in Hawaii to do it.

Thursday morning dawned hot and smoggy. Kate put on her suit and took Bonny out for a swim. The cool water soothed, and Bonny's squeals of delight helped to improve her mother's mood. They were sunning together on a blanket when the phone brought Kate out of her reverie. Bill Teasdale's Queen's English on the line surprised her.

"I hope all's well, Kate."

"Things are fine. What can I do for you, Bill?"

"Kate, I've just heard from Scotland Yard. There has been a break in the Beale case."

Kate sat up, moved the phone to her other ear.

"A witness has come forward, on the condition of anonymity, and has deposed that he saw two additional men outside the Flynn property just after Paul and Jon walked down the street."

"Really?" Kate asked, the shock evident in her voice. "Did they say who it was?"

"One of the men was none other than Ian Flynn himself. The other, an unidentified man wearing a hooded windbreaker.

No way to see his face, especially in the dark. So the detectives are questioning Flynn and keeping him under surveillance."

"Good grief. Does Paul know?"

"Yes. I've just spoken with him. He's quite concerned."

"He should be concerned. Damn."

"I'm not really involved, dear, but as an interested party, I'm somewhat privy to what goes on. I felt you should know. I've always considered Mr. Flynn with disdain. He's an unsavory type, and I guarantee you he is no friend of your ex-husband."

"Indeed," Kate murmured. "What's going to happen? Is there any way to get more information on the other man?"

"The witness says he did not come from the party, but from elsewhere outside. The two men talked, and then the hooded one followed the same path Paul made, until the witness could no longer see in the darkness. He also said that Flynn watched for a bit and then returned to the house."

"And why didn't this person come forward sooner?"

"Fear, most likely. He's currently in a secret witness protection program."

"I see."

"And Kate, I don't mean to alarm you, but the Yard has reason to suspect that the mystery person might currently be residing in the U.S. In... Southern California."

"How do they know that?"

"One of those facts I'm not privy to. But Kip is fairly adept at getting information out of them. We'll see."

"Thank you, Bill. I appreciate the heads-up. Do you think...is Paulie safe?"

"What I believe is, had this person wanted to kill Paulie, he would have done so straight out. No reason to set up Jon, murder him, plant evidence and all that rot. He is a soulless killer, however. Mind that you keep your doors and windows locked. Keep Rob close at hand, will you?"

"Sure. Of course. Please keep me informed."

Kate wasted no time in dialing Paulie's number. The phone barely rang.

"I was just going to call you. You spoke with Teasdale?"

"Yes. Paul, I'm worried about you."

"Me? You're the one I'm concerned for. I'm booking a flight for you and Bonny."

"I can't just leave."

"If you won't come here, then I'm coming there."

"Come if you want. You know how much I'd like to see you, but it's not necessary, really. We're safe here."

"Yeah, with a boyfriend who won't even stay with you at night."

"He doesn't know about this yet. I called you first."

Paulie was quiet. Kate could visualize his face as he thought about her words. "Tell him. Then I want you to pack your goddam bags and let him take you out to Shambala or whatever the hell he calls that place. Do you understand?"

"Do you really think..."

Kate heard Paulie sigh. *He's getting angry.* It tickled her, in a way.

"Listen carefully, Katrina. Listen to my words and pretend, for a moment, that I still have some wee bit of power. Remember what it was like when you believed in me, believed in what I said, and if anything still matters between us, you will do as I say. I saw, in ungodly large color photos, what this man is capable of doing. Now we can mince words all day and play at guessing what's going on in each other's lives, but unless you give me your promise that you will do this, I'm going to call Rob and give him instructions on what he needs to do and how he's supposed to take care of you."

Kate drew in a shaky breath, watched Bonny kick her feet in the pool water.

"Okay. I promise."

"Believe this, darling. You know I'm a risk-taker. But I will never see you or Bonny harmed. I have to be assured. Will you have Rob call me when you are locked in?"

"Yes, Paul. I will."

"I will be back in L.A. soon, it's just a matter of when. Scotland Yard wants to interview me."

"An interview? How fun. Will you be in drag?"

Kate was a risk-taker, too, and this particular risk paid off as she heard Paulie chuckling on the phone.

"Cheeky little witch."

Chapter 7

July 28, 1995.

Even though she thought it was entirely unnecessary, Kate complied with Paulie's wishes, packing up a few days' worth of clothing and toys. Rob, of course, was annoyingly supportive of the idea, and Kate tried not to fault him for it. The issue added weight to his side of the seesaw.

Cheryl was on location at the Los Angeles County Arboretum, shooting peacocks and flowers and fountains. Not her favorite work, but it was a good foot in the door at *Sunset Magazine*. Kate left an abridged version of the fire drill on Cheryl's voicemail and finished loading her car.

They were almost ready to leave when Bonny took a tumble on the front porch. A nasty gash on her knee necessitated some love and bandages, so Kate carried the bawling girl back inside and sat her on the bottom riser of the stairs, then grabbed the first aid kit from the bathroom.

"It will only hurt for a little while, Bon. Be brave for Mommy, okay?"

Bonny nodded tearfully while Kate tore open the small bandage strips adorned with Rainbow Brite. She called Rob while she worked, to let him know she was on her way, and then hurriedly swept Bonny up and out to the car.

He was standing on the front porch with a hunting rifle in his hands. Alarmed at first, Kate got the joke when she saw his grin.

"You're gonna protect me with that puny thing? Where's the AK-47?"

"In the bedroom," he said. "I put it in there after that night you beat me up."

Nick approached, nodded at Kate.

"I asked Nick and Sarah to move into the bunkhouse for a while," Rob explained.

"Works out well, good time for me to get my roof redone," Nick assured her.

Kate nodded. All this trouble, just because of some hunch.

Nick helped Rob unload Kate's trunk. Bonny pranced about, kicking at rocks.

"See my new boots, Rob? I'm a cowgirl now. An' Mummy and me are gonna stay at your house now."

"Those new boots betrayed her on the front porch." Kate gestured toward the bandaged knee.

"She'll get used to them. All cowgirls do."

They started for the house, when Kate slapped her right front pocket, then the others, in succession. She trotted back to the car, leaned in.

"Crap. I don't have my phone." She pawed through her shoulder bag, looked on the floor of the backseat. "Rob, I have to go back. I need my phone. I must have left it when Bonny got hurt."

"Do you really need it that bad?"

Kate looked away, pushed a lock of hair behind her ear. "Yeah. It's my only way of reaching Paul. He probably doesn't have your number, and I don't know his by heart. It'll only take an hour. I'll hurry."

"Let me go."

"No. I need you to stay here with Bonny. Please."

Rob sighed, shoved his hands into the front pockets of his jeans. "I won't win anyway, so no sense in arguing. Call me when you find it."

Kate hated to drive all the way back home, but knew without her phone she'd be miserable. Paulie was waiting to hear from her. His and Alec's phone numbers were a matter of British national security; no one had them.

Driving down Sunset, she checked the time on her dashboard: 4:45 p.m. Cheryl had probably called her by now. But as she turned into the driveway, she was happy to see Cheryl's Ford Mustang parked in the garage. She hurried into the house.

"Cher?"

No answer. Kate started to pick up the forgotten box of bandages and antiseptic when she heard a noise upstairs. "Cheryl?"

She quickly climbed the stairs and headed for her cousin's bedroom. "You won't believe what's going on. I got a call... Cher? Where are you?"

Cheryl's room was empty. Kate went on, peeked quickly into Bonny's vacant room before continuing on to her own at the end of the hall. She was stopped cold by the sight of a man standing at her dresser, his back to her. He was wearing a long black coat, despite the warm weather outside. In his hand was the framed wedding photo from her dresser.

"Lovely picture."

He turned, and Kate drew in a gasp.

"How did you get in here?" she managed to say. She grasped the doorframe and the man smiled, then held up a set of keys from which dangled a small silver replica of a Nikon camera.

Cheryl's keys.

"Don't tell me you're... Stan?"

"How astute, Katrina."

"You're not welcome here. Please leave."

"Why, of course. I only came to pick you up, anyway."

☙ *Fortunately, I still had Rob's phone number from when we visited in March. I was getting anxious, couldn't wait any longer. It was 2:30 a.m., but Alec and I were still up, as usual. Alec seemed annoyed, but I dialed anyway. Rob was in his car, heading out to Kate's place because she'd not checked in or returned. Apparently, she left her phone behind and had gone back to retrieve it.*

By the time he called back, I'd already had a plane ticket reserved. He was at the house, Kate was missing. Her car was there, as was her phone. But there was evidence of a possible struggle, he said, something about a smashed picture frame, broken glass, the bedside phone on the floor. The police, he said, were already there. He was nearly falling apart as he spoke. I'd never seen or heard him like that before.

I, of course, went ballistic. Knowing Kate's stubbornness, I could hardly blame Rob. Nonetheless, she'd been abducted and neither of us was there to protect her.

I was agitated and surly on the plane. Couldn't sleep. Six hours into the flight I popped a couple of sleeping pills, and nodded off for a fitful nap. I was angry and antagonistic when we landed in Los Angeles. Alec should have been with me to run interference. I was nearly arrested.

Rob had a driver waiting for me. The news people were already reporting Kate's disappearance on the radio. I worked on my attitude in the car, because I knew that's what Kate would want. It wouldn't do to mouth off at Rob, although I wanted badly to blame him.

I'd never seen Cheryl cry before. Her eyes were red and swollen, streaks of dark mascara running down her cheeks. Rob was pacing like a caged lion. I took one look at them both and walked on through to the room where Bonny's laughter cascaded like liquid sugar.

"Daddy! Daddy! Daddy!"

"Bonny, my precious." Paulie held his daughter tightly, breathing in the candy sweet smell of her, absorbing her strength. "How's my best girl?"

"This is my little girl room at Rob's house. I have a big box of toys, see?"

"Wonderful, sweetheart."

There was a young woman sitting on the bed, an open story book in her lap. She held out her hand. "Sarah Valente. My husband is Nick. He's in the band."

"Pleased. Paul Bingham. I'm Bonny's father."

The woman smiled. "We were just reading about Horton the Elephant. Bonny, Daddy probably needs to get unpacked and stuff."

"Okay. Come back Daddy."

"I will Bon. Give me a bit to get settled."

He made his way back to the great room where he stood, awkwardly, waiting for someone to speak.

"Any news?"

"No."

Paulie sat down. "How long has it been?"

"Sometime between 4:30 and 6:00 p.m. yesterday."

Paulie looked at the clock over the mantel. It was just after noon. "No bloody clues at all?"

Rob sighed, ran his hands through his already disheveled hair. "I got there at around 7. Kate's car was parked in the driveway, so I thought she was there. The front door was unlocked. I went in, looked around. There was a box of Band-Aids and some Bactine on the stairs, Bonny had taken a tumble before they left and she'd fixed her up. She thought that was why she forgot the phone. I looked around, went upstairs. In the bedroom, the picture was smashed on the dresser. The rug, you know that little green rug next to the dresser? It was all messed up. The phone from the nightstand was on the floor, off the hook. Her cell was on the floor. That's it."

Paulie stared at Rob. Tried to envision what Rob had seen.

"What picture?"

"The wedding picture. You. Her. At the beach. It was busted, glass all over the place."

"Where's her phone?"

"They took it. The cops. And the photo. And the desk phone."

Paulie drew in a deep breath. "You should have been with her."

Both Cheryl and Rob looked at him.

"You know how she is. She insisted I stay here with Bonny. I couldn't argue with her."

Paulie shook his head. "Didn't she explain the danger she was in? I should have called you myself."

"She explained. But I got that she wasn't taking it that seriously. She doesn't want to stay here."

"And you don't want to stay there. Great relationship. Brilliant future you two have, living across town from each other."

Rob raised his eyebrows in surprise. Cheryl lowered her head. Paulie stood up.

"And you damn well could have argued with her. Taken her fucking keys out of her hand. What were you thinking, man?

A little girl like that is no match for the kind of animal that killed Jon."

Cheryl lifted her head. "Oh, for crying out loud, Paul, just stuff it. Your throwing a God damned tantrum isn't going to help Kate!"

Rob shook his head. "No, Cher. He's right. I could have stopped her somehow. I wasn't thinking. I didn't realize what was really going on. She said Teasdale said there was a hunch that maybe the accomplice was in So Cal. That's all we knew, and we only knew that yesterday afternoon. Just hours before she was taken. It didn't seem that imminent. But I blew it, and I'm—I'm dying inside because of it."

Paulie turned away. "Did the police have anything else to say?"

"They dusted everything. I was waiting in the driveway when the cab came up. I prayed, for an instant, that Kate would get out, but it was Cheryl. The cops asked lots of questions, I told them everything I knew. I gave them details about the murder investigation in London. They said they would check it out. Cheryl went in and grabbed some clothes and Bonny's food and then we came back here. We haven't slept."

Paulie turned to Cheryl. "Why the cab?"

"My car is in the shop."

"The door was unlocked, no signs of forced entry. All the other doors were locked up tight. So whoever came in either had a key, or she let them in." Rob was pacing again. "Unless she left the door open when she went looking for her phone."

"I can't imagine she'd do that. She's too careful," Cheryl said. "She's accidentally locked me out twice when I was taking out the trash. She's a nut about locking doors."

"True," Paulie agreed. "So who else has a key?"

Cheryl shook back her hair. "Uh, there's a cleaning lady that comes in once a month, but—no; she gave the key back last month because she was going to Mexico for a while. Evelyn used a key while she and Pop were here, but I'm pretty sure they left it. There's a little nook drawer in the—"

"—kitchen. Yes. I know." Paulie nodded. Rob flashed him a raw look.

Cheryl sighed. "That leaves just me and you, if you still have yours."

Paulie fished a set of keys out of his pocket, held them up. "Souvenir. Where is yours?"

"At the Ford dealer on La Cienega. They have my whole key ring there. I don't usually do that, but...well, Stan dropped it off for me, after he took me to Arcadia for the shoot. He works near the dealership. When I got Kate's message, I left the park and took a cab back."

"Who is Stan?"

"A guy I'm seeing."

"Really. Didn't know."

Rob frowned. "So...Stan had your keys?"

"Only until he dropped off the Mustang, of course. The Ford place has them now. I just checked, the car won't be ready until tomorrow."

Paulie pressed his fist against his forehead. "Alec is pressuring Scotland Yard to bring Ian in for interrogation. They need to twist his fucking arms off until he tells."

"Are they pretty sure he's involved?"

"Teasdale seems to think so. I gave a statement before I left. Nothing very detailed. They wouldn't divulge anything to me."

"How did they figure there was someone over here?" Rob asked.

Paulie shook his head. "Kip overheard something about phone records. There was also an airline ticket stub torn in half, found near where Ian puts out his rubbish. It was dated a few days before the murder."

Rob walked to the door. "I need some air. I'll be out back."

When he'd gone, Paulie went to Cheryl and held out his hands. She stood, and he embraced her.

"I'm glad you're here, Paul. We have to be strong," she whispered through her sobs. "It wasn't really Rob's fault."

"I know. I know. We'll get her back, somehow. She's too important to too many people."

They ate dinner that night at the big trestle table in the dining room, with Nick and Sarah joining them. After complaints about the heat and speculation over its duration, conversation dropped off, except for Bonny's four-year-old views on the world and whether or not she could still eat meat if Daddy was watching.

Rob showed Paulie to the one of the four empty bedrooms. Paulie tossed his bag onto the bed.

"Look, Rob, I'm sorry for what I said. No one is a bigger asshole than I am. Somehow, I am behind all this madness, I just don't know why."

Rob shook his head.

"Will you be up for a while?" Paulie ventured.

"I'm wasted. But...wired. I might sit outside for a while. It's finally cooled off. Come on out if you want, but don't be spooked if I partake. Kate told me you don't do it anymore."

Paulie gave him a half smile. "There are some things Kate doesn't need to know. I'm going to spend a wee bit of time with Bonny. Don't smoke it all, mate."

Stars pelleted the sky. Paulie leaned back in the chaise lounge, stared up at the celestial glitter. Rob's pot was smooth, and he felt his body relax. Beside him, Rob sat in the matching chair.

"Bonny asked me when Mummy was coming home," Paulie muttered.

"What did you say?"

"I told her that she was on a wee vacation, and would be home soon. Soon usually works."

"She breaks my heart."

"Every day," Paulie agreed. "She is the most precious gift ever given."

The sound of the crickets seemed louder in the silence between them. Rob relit a joint, then passed it to Paulie. Paulie took a toke, then chuckled.

"What's so funny?"

"I was just imagining what Kate would do if she walked up right now and caught us doing this."

Rob stared, then smiled. Then laughed. "Shit, yeah. She would beat us senseless."

Paulie nodded.

When their laughter had died away, Rob rubbed his eyes. "What are we gonna do, Paul?"

"I was just thinking the same thing. I wish I knew."

Chapter 8

July 30, 1995. Los Angeles, CA

Paulie got up and dressed by nine. He found Rob already in the kitchen drinking black coffee.

"Any word?"

"Nope."

"I have a favor to ask. Is there a car I could borrow?"

"Cars all over the place. Are you taking off?"

"I want to go to the house."

Rob peered at Paulie over his steaming cup. "Want company? I can drive."

Cheryl asked for a ride to the Ford dealer, and the three of them left Bonny in the care of the Valentes.

Despite the heat, or maybe because of it, they opted to put the top down and cruised east on the Ventura Freeway. The noise level made conversation impractical, which was just okay with them all, Paulie decided. After dropping Cheryl off, they continued on into Brentwood.

When Rob pulled the BMW to a stop on Kate's driveway, Paulie's stomach rolled. Kate's white convertible was still parked just outside the closed garage door. He'd all but forgotten the day he'd taken her out to buy it, the same day he'd left the house to start a new life without her.

They pulled away the yellow police tape, stood awkwardly on the porch together.

"I'm the one without a key," Rob murmured, and Paulie quickly pulled his from his pocket, unlocked the door. Before they could get inside, a photographer appeared from nowhere, snapping pictures of the two of them together. Paulie slammed the door shut in his face.

"That should make for a nice front page spread, eh?" he asked Rob.

Rob didn't answer. He went to the living room and sat down. Paulie paused at the bottom of the stairs.

"I won't be long. I just want to look around. You know."

"Sure. Take your time."

Paulie went immediately to Kate's bedroom. Formerly, their bedroom. Bits of broken glass still littered the dresser and the floor.

He wandered slowly around the room, catching memories. He opened his nightstand drawer, found a handful of foil-wrapped condoms. His. In the bathroom, he looked into the medicine cabinet, shook his head at the after shave, the razors, the deodorant. All his.

The closet stood open. Empty hangers where she'd taken clothes to pack. On his side, a handful of garments left behind. A pair of shoes. Two hats. He covered his eyes with his hand for a moment, tried to breathe.

When his father died, his mother did the same thing. Left everything exactly as it was the day he collapsed in the factory, where he repaired aircraft engine parts. Paulie had always found it unsettling, seeing his father's things around when he clearly wasn't coming back.

Kate wasn't that morose. Her reasons for keeping his stuff were entirely different. He sensed her, channeled her very thoughts; he wasn't dead, thank God, and just maybe, he would be back someday.

His sadness increased tenfold.

No wonder Rob refused to sleep in the *Paulie Bingham Tribute Room.*

With the air off for days, the house was unbearably hot. Paulie went back downstairs and to the refrigerator. "Bless her," he said aloud, pulling out two bottles of Amstel. He took one to Rob, held it out to him. In the reach, his long-sleeve t-shirt cuff rode up, exposing the new tattoo.

Rob stared at Paulie's wrist, then back at his face. "Nice tat."

Paulie shrugged. "You must think me the world's biggest fool."

Rob opened the beer, took a long drink. "Second only to me."

"Do you think it was wrong of me to come?"

"I'd have been shocked and disappointed if you hadn't." Rob stood up, walked a few steps. "I don't know if you're aware of it, but Kate's been..." he shook his head, propped his foot on the fireplace hearth, "depressed. Pretty much since we got back, after the trial. I don't know what happened, I don't even think I want to know, but if—when we get her back, I plan to do everything I can to fix it."

"How can I help?"

"You know how you can help."

Paulie chewed his bottom lip, knowing it would bleed. He looked up at Rob. "You understand I can't leave until I know she's safe."

"I've hoped, all along, that this wouldn't come between us."

"This? You mean Kate?"

Rob nodded, sat back down. "I don't know if I can compete, Paul. You lift an eyebrow, and she's rapt. You moan, she coddles. You take up with someone new, she worries about your happiness."

"That's what friends do."

"No. It's not just friendship."

"I've never tried to stand in your way, Ev. Quite the contrary. I've encouraged her to pursue a relationship with you. I can't control everything she does. Or at least, I certainly don't try to."

Paulie felt his usual nausea settle in. He wanted to run, like he'd been caught by the headmaster at school. Despite his earlier assertion, Rob Evans was no fool.

They sat in silence while they drank, until Rob's cellular phone rang. Rob listened intently, Paulie watched. After ending the call, Rob slammed down his beer and stood up. "Let's go. They found her."

"Alive?"

Rob nodded. "But not conscious. She's at St. Joe's. It's about twenty minutes away."

The ten miles to St. Joseph's Hospital seemed more like a hundred as Paulie held tight to the door handle of Rob's BMW. Rob parked in the emergency lot, and the two men rushed inside, to be met by a detective waiting at the information desk. They were shown to a small meeting room.

"Mr. Evans, Mr. Bingham, Tom Callahan, L.A.P.D. I've asked Dr. Walters to join us, he'll be here soon. Let's sit down."

Rob and the detective sat, but Paulie was too nervous to do anything but stand and try not to wring his hands.

"I'm sorry to have to ask this, but are either of you currently married to Ms. Bingham?"

The two men looked at each other, shook their heads.

"I see. I believe her parents are en route from New Mexico."

"Just tell us, is she okay?" Paulie asked.

"Not really. She's pretty rough. But I'll let the doctor explain all that. So, since I don't really know whom to ask, I'll have to ask you both. Does the victim have any history of drug abuse?"

"No," Rob said.

"Absolutely not." Paulie affirmed. "She will barely take a goddam aspirin."

"Why do you ask?" Rob wanted to know.

"Because she was pumped full of heroin."

Paulie took a step backward, clutched at his throat. "No."

"Then somebody did that to her. She'd never even consider that," Rob said. "Wow. I can't...I can't..."

An older physician wearing surgical scrubs came briskly into the room.

"Ah. Dr. Walters. These gentlemen are the victim's friends."

"I can speak freely?"

"Yes. We are overriding HIPAA rules here."

"I'm sorry, I only have a couple of minutes. The patient had been restrained. She's suffered multiple bruises, contusions. One or two bruised ribs, a four centimeter laceration on her right, no, left temple required stitches. Her right ankle is bruised, probably sprained. She has been injected with heroin, we don't know how much; we're waiting on additional toxicology reports. She's still nodding."

Rob spoke up first. "Does that mean she's in a coma?"

"No, she's in a deep, dream-like consciousness. However, her central nervous system is extremely depressed, likely due to the heroin. There's brain activity, and she'll likely emerge into a more wakeful state soon. I could administer naloxone which would wake her up in a hurry, but again, I want to see labs first."

Paulie had paced away while the doctor spoke, but now returned and leaned onto the table with both hands. "Was she sexually assaulted?"

Dr. Walters gave Paulie a level stare. "There is evidence of possible penetration with a foreign object."

Rob looked away. "How do you know she was restrained?"

"There are injuries consistent with being chained, or wired, on her arms and ankles."

"Son of a bitch," Rob murmured.

"If that's all, I need to get to the OR."

"Can we see her?" Paulie asked.

"Yes. But be forewarned. She's battered."

The doctor left the detective with Paulie and Rob, both too stunned to speak.

"I have questions for you two. But they can wait until after."

Outside the intensive care ward, Paulie waved Rob ahead. "You go. You're present. I'm past."

"No you're not."

"Go."

Rob went inside, and Paulie sat down in a chair. He'd been fighting stomach problems all day. He was afraid to go in, afraid to see her, but he clearly couldn't wait, either. They could have gone in together, but Paulie wanted to see her alone.

It wasn't long before Rob came out, his eyes red-rimmed and angry. He walked to the opposite wall, gestured behind his back for Paulie to go in.

Paulie's breath caught in his throat at the sight of her. She looked so small, childlike, nearly swallowed by the white, sterile hospital bed around her. Her hair was cut very short, not unlike his own. A large bandage covered one side of her forehead. There were various tubes and needles connected to her. Beeps and blips from machines. A nurse busied herself nearby.

He took Kate's hand. It was so tiny, so warm. The same hand that had worn his ring. Had massaged his neck, slapped his face, touched his body. He squeezed it, but she did not squeeze back.

Paulie glanced at the nurse. "Miss? Do you know...do you know if her hair, did they cut it like this for a reason?"

"I was here when they brought her in. It was already like that. I would have thought she was a young boy, if her eyes hadn't been all smudged up with eye makeup."

Paulie touched Kate's cheek, a feather touch, so as not to startle her. He leaned down, kissed her mouth. He wondered, fleetingly, if Rob had done the same. It didn't matter. Tears fell onto her face. He got down on his knees, bowed his head.

"Dear Lord, I've been a fuck-up all my life, we both know that, and You might as well also know that I'm not even sure you exist. But if You do, and you can see your way clear, please help me. I need to know what I've done and how to fix this and stop this nightmare. She didn't deserve this, and You know damn well that I would never do anything to hurt her. But somehow, this is my fault, and I don't even know why. So I'm asking, not for me, but for her and Jon all the others who are hurt by this. Give me a clue, please. I need your help." He paused to dab at his eyes with his sleeve.

"And it's okay if you want Rob to have her. I will go away and never bother them, if that's your will. Only just please bring her back, and help me bring whoever did this to judgment.

"Just a clue. A sign."

The nurse was sniffing. Paulie stood, and again lowered his lips to Kate's. He lingered, feeling her breath on his cheek. "I love you, Kate. Please come back."

He started to straighten up when her lips moved.

"Paulie." It was the tiniest whimper of a word, and yet she remained still. He turned quickly.

"Did you hear that? Did you?"

The nurse nodded. "She said something. Yes. They do that sometimes, like people who talk in their sleep. I couldn't make it out, though."

"She said my name."

"Perhaps. It may have just been a sigh."

He returned to the waiting room. Rob didn't look at all well.

"What do we do now?" Paulie asked.

"That cop wants to talk to us."

"Did you call Cheryl, by chance?"

Rob nodded. "She's on her way down here right now. You okay?"

"Not particularly. But I'm a helluva lot better than when I thought she might be dead."

"Yeah."

They answered questions for the better part of an hour. Paulie took time out to call Alec, and then William Teasdale. Cheryl arrived, and Rob volunteered to pick up Kate's parents at nearby Burbank Airport. Paulie was glad; Rob's anxiety only made his own worse.

He and Cheryl went to the cafeteria for a bite to eat.

"She looks terrible," Cheryl said.

"She looks like an angel to me."

"Yeah, well, you always did have stars in your eyes. When did you get the tat? It looks fresh."

"A couple of weeks ago."

"Rob see that?"

"Unfortunately, yes."

"And how does Alec feel about you inking your ex-wife's name on your wrist?"

"It's my wrist. And Alec knows Kate has been my closest friend for twelve years. It has no bearing on our relationship. Besides, it hides a scar, it's permanent, nothing I can do about it, now."

"I have a tiger on my ass," Cheryl commented, taking a bite out of her club sandwich.

"Ask me if I'm surprised."

"What was the scar from?"

Paulie shrugged. "An old injury. No big deal. I just didn't like it. You know how vain I am."

Cheryl reached across him for the ketchup. His eyes were drawn to her wrist, and a silver bracelet bearing a single charm.

She held it out. "I bought one like this for Kate for her birthday, and then got myself a matching one," she explained. Paulie took her hand, turned it to examine the bracelet. And beneath the shiny silver links, he saw something else. A scar, not unlike his own.

"You have one, too."

"Duh, didn't I just explain?"

"No, I mean, the scar. You have one too. Just like the one I had."

"Oh. That. I was playing around with a set of handcuffs. Got pinched. Long time ago. Like you said, no big deal."

"Handcuffs, eh? It doesn't look that old. Into a little bondage, are we?"

"Shut up."

Paulie laughed, release her hand.

They waited for Kate's parents together. Evelyn rushed up to Cheryl, collapsed into her arms. When she calmed somewhat, she turned to Paulie and hugged him, then Rob. The process was repeated with Pop.

Cheryl took her aunt and uncle in to see Kate while Paulie took the time to call and check on his daughter. Rob approached him.

"Everything okay at home?"

"Yeah. They're collecting eggs or some such nonsense."

"Would it be wrong for me to go home for a while?"

Paulie placed his hand on Rob's shoulder. "It would be absolutely fine for you to go home. Nothing is happening here. I'll go with Cheryl to get Mum and Pop settled into the hotel, and then we'll be along. They'll call us if she wakes up or anything."

"Are you sure?"

"Yes. You go, tell Bonny I'll be home soon."

Rob hesitated, then engulfed Paulie in a man embrace. "We'll get through this, man. We will."

By 8:00 p.m., Paulie could see the strain was getting to Evelyn.

"We need to get Mum to bed," he whispered to Cheryl, who nodded. "I'm going to say goodnight to Kate."

He entered her room one last time for the night. She had not moved. The nurse looked in.

"Going home, soon, Mr. Bingham?"

"Yeah. I'll be of more use after I've had some rest." He stood looking down at Kate, his adoring eyes taking in every detail, every feature.

"Sleep well, my love." He lifted her hand to his lips. "So soft," he whispered, drawing his fingers lightly down her arm, pausing to marvel at the size of her small wrist. And he frowned, because there was a butterfly bandage stretched across a small laceration.

"I didn't notice that before."

"What's that, dear?"

"This cut. I missed seeing it before."

"It's painful to see those we love injured."

"What do you suppose made that cut?"

"Hard to say. The police likely have already speculated." The nurse touched his arm. "You'd best get on home. Your daughter will be missing you, especially with her mother gone."

"You know about our daughter?"

"Why, of course. Everyone knows. It's all over the news, the radio, the papers. The hospital has been sending folks away all day. There's a whole room full of flowers downstairs."

He hadn't thought. Kate had been found, but the monster who'd harmed her and killed Jon was still out there. Bonny was still in danger, as was Rob, Cheryl, Evelyn and Pop. Even Alec. Because whoever had committed these heinous acts was doing it to hurt Paulie, it was now clear.

☞ *From Rob: They found her in Griffith Park at 5:30 in the morning. She was only wearing a thin, tattered man's shirt and a pair of short boy's pants. You wouldn't know her to look at her, she looked like a young boy, her hair was all cut off with an electric hair cutter. She was battered, beaten, broken. Needle marks in her arm, smack in her veins. I know Paulie felt the same way I did, sick and yet murderous. Either of us would have become killers ourselves that day, given the chance.*

I took a double hit. When I went into her room, I was just shattered by her appearance. I was afraid to touch her, afraid it would hurt her somehow. She seemed so fragile, like a china doll. But worst of all was that she turned her head, ever so slightly, and uttered a word. It was so soft, I can't be sure. But if I had to guess, I'd have to say that the word was "Paul."

I don't know what comes next. She'll recover, with luck and prayers. But what then? Do I keep trying to blunder my way into her heart? You know, I'd just give in if I truly thought they were right for each other, but they aren't.

Paul dallies in a fantasy world, ping-ponging around like a pinball. He has her name tatted on his arm.

—Rob Evans, #2

Chapter 9

Sunday, July 31, 1995.

Paulie woke early. Rob, he discovered, had already gone back to St. Joseph's, so he took his time getting ready to go. He spent some time with Bonny, let her take him on a brief tour of the chicken coop. They rested on a rustic wooden bench, and he drew her onto his lap.

"Bonny, I need to tell you something. Mummy's had a wee accident, and she had to go to the hospital."

Bonny's eyes grew round. "Is she okay? Does she got a broken bone?"

"Not broken, but she does have a sore place. Right here," he said poking her gently in the ribs. Bonny couldn't help but giggle, and he hugged her close, rocking her as she laughed.

"Can I go see her?" Bonny asked, when her giggles had subsided.

"Maybe. I'll find out, okay? She needs to get lots of sleepy time, so she can get better. But she said to tell you she loves you and she'll be home soon, okay?"

"Okay. I love Mummy, too."

Sarah Valente approached. "There you are, you little scamp! Daddy stole you away!"

"Sorry. Should've mentioned."

Sarah smiled. "Naw. I saw you two slip out. I was only kidding. Is this young lady up for some flapjacks this morning?"

Bonny clapped her hands, then took Paulie's face between them. "That's pancakes, Daddy. Want some?"

"Maybe later, Bon. Right now, I'm going to go see Mummy."

He'd picked up Kate's car, figuring he might as well use it and not be dependent upon rides from Cheryl or Rob.

The sun was already blazing. He stopped at Cheryl's Mustang and peered inside in search of his sunglasses. She'd left the car unlocked, so he slipped into the passenger seat where he'd sat yesterday, and looked around. His glasses were on the console. He was just getting out when he noticed something reflecting from the floor. A silver bracelet. He remembered Cheryl showing it to him the day before. He took it inside.

Cheryl wasn't around, so he left the bracelet on the kitchen counter and mentioned it to Sarah before heading out.

Rob and Cheryl had picked up Kate's parents and were chatting with them in the second floor waiting room. Rob stood up when Paulie walked in.

"Sorry, didn't want to wake you," he told Paulie.

"No worries. I spent some time with Bonny this morning. Have you been in to see Kate?"

"Yeah. No change."

Paulie nodded. He turned to Evelyn and Pop. "You sleep well?"

"Pop went right out, it's his medication, you know. But I fretted half the night. I just tossed and turned."

Paulie leaned down and kissed her cheek. "Don't worry, Mum. She'll be okay." He turned back to Rob. "I'm going to go see her now."

He sat beside Kate the better part of the day. Sometimes chatting with her, sometimes just watching her. He thrilled to the slightest stirring. The doctors and nurses came and went, and Paulie charmed them all.

Rob joined him for a while, then Kate's parents stayed in the room while he and Rob grabbed a quick snack in the cafeteria. They made small talk, speculated about what could happen next. They were just finishing their food when Cheryl appeared and slid into the booth beside Rob.

"I need to get home," she muttered. "This waiting is wigging me out. There's no need for us all to be mooning around. Aunt Eve said they want to stay longer. Pop will get them a taxi back to their room."

"I'll take you home," Rob offered.

"Yeah, I promised Bonny I'd be home early tonight," Paulie agreed. "Let's go."

They sat in the living room together, Cheryl on the floor, fiddling with one of her cameras.

"Found your bracelet, I see," Paulie remarked.

Cheryl held up her wrist. "It wasn't lost."

"No, I mean, I found it on the floor of your car. I put it on the counter."

"That wasn't mine. It must be Kate's."

"Oh." Paulie nodded. "I'd forgotten you said they were identical. She must have dropped it in your car?"

Rob frowned. "Uh, no."

"What do you mean?" Paulie asked.

"She was wearing her bracelet when she went back to the house for her phone. When she was taken."

Paulie froze, stared hard at Rob's concerned face. "Are you certain?"

"Absolutely certain. She got Bonny out of the car. Bonny was dancing around, showing off her new boots. Kate told me Bonny had pitched on the front porch...then...she started looking for her cell phone. She was doing one of these," he demonstrated by feeling his front, then back pockets, "and I remember seeing that bracelet flashing in the sunlight."

Both men turned to Cheryl, who was now sitting up straight, alert.

"But how the hell did it get into my car?"

Paulie got up, retrieved the bracelet from the counter, and held it near the light. "This is hers. ' Cher to Kate'." He swallowed, moistened his lips. "I need to ask you something important."

Cheryl tilted her head. "Okay."

"When we were talking about the bracelets, you said you got that scar on your wrist from playing with handcuffs."

"Yeah, so? My habits can't be any more perverted than yours. You said you had the same scar."

"And Kate has the same injury on her wrist."

"What the hell are you talking about, Paul?" Rob demanded.

"I'm thinking the same person is responsible for all of this. What's your boyfriend's name again? The one who had your car?"

"This is crazy. Stan's a sweetheart. He'd never do anything to hurt Kate or anyone else."

"Stan?" Paulie turned to Rob. "Have you ever met this guy?"

"Never. He's never been around when Kate and I are there."

Cheryl bristled. "It's purely coincidental. You're off your nut, Bingham."

"Did you describe him to me, Cheryl?"

"No, I don't think I did."

"Okay. Let me. He's a Brit. About 5-8, thirteen stone, shaved head, piercing blue eyes...possibly a goatee. And a small tattoo on his neck. It's a dragon."

Cheryl frowned, clearly becoming upset. "I must have told you."

"And he tied you up, didn't he?" Paulie pressed his palm to his forehead. "I am one stupid git. Stanton. David Stanton."

"Someone you know?" Rob asked.

"I need to call Callahan. Do you have a picture of him? This...Stan?" Paulie asked Cheryl, who'd turned ghost white.

"Yes...but not here. In my other camera, at home."

"Never mind," Paulie said, digging out his cell phone. "It should be easy to get a photo of him. He was with Bingham Boys for two years. Christ! I can't believe I didn't think of him before. I even had them drag in that heathen Goff."

Rob shook his head. "What about the wrist thing? Did he do that to you?"

Paulie, now sitting on the ottoman, looked up at Rob as he waited for his call to connect to L.A.P.D. "Yeah. He did." He closed his eyes, unable to bear Rob's questioning gaze. "Detective Callahan? Paul Bingham. I have the name of Kate's abductor."

The investigator and his assistant arrived at Rob's ranch thirty minutes later. Cheryl's hands were shaking as she held a wine glass to her lips.

"Do you have an address for this man, Miss Collins?"

"He has a ticket for London in the morning," she muttered. "He was going on business. Government business."

"The address, please?"

"He used to live in Malibu," Paulie offered.

Cheryl recalled Stanton's apartment address in Universal City. "He never said anything about a beach house."

Rob, who'd left the room, returned with a vinyl LP record album cover. He turned it over, handed it to Paulie. "This him?"

"Yeah, that's the bastard." He turned a surprised eye to Rob. "You have this? You actually bought this?"

"No accounting for taste, I guess." Rob managed a brief smile. "It's not half-bad, actually."

Callahan looked up. "I have it, too." He turned back to Cheryl. "So, do you believe the suspect is still in town?"

"I spoke with him this afternoon. I'll give you his telephone number. Oh, God...I just can't believe this. To think that Stan did those horrible things to Kate...he used me. Used me to get to her. It's just so sick."

Rob put his arm around Cheryl.

Callahan got on the phone and issued an APB for David Stanton, alias Stan Davidson. "We were able to get a fairly recent photo of the guy from the gym where you met him," he told Cheryl after hanging up.

"I should've thought of that," she murmured.

The detective touched her shoulder. "I'm sorry, Miss Collins. If it's any consolation, the last girl I dated, I met at an art gallery. I thought she was pretty cool until I found out she was wanted in two states for grand larceny."

Cheryl nodded slowly, still distracted by her shock.

"He was going after Alec next." Paulie shook his head. As hard as he tried to dispel them, images of his night in hell kept emerging. Spiked, handcuff-like wrist restraints that tightened the more he struggled. Whips, small, knotted chains, disguised with feathers, wrapped in velvet and silk. Blindfolds, belts. Buckles, ropes, twisted wires and all manners of fake penises.

"This man is inhumanly perverted and vile," he said quietly to Callahan. "You must get him and make this stick. He must never ever be free again."

The detective gave him a pointed look. "Do you have charges to press, too, Mr. Bingham?"

Both Cheryl and Rob waited for Paulie's response.

"No."

The three of them waited together for the call, which came approximately one hour later. It was 11 p.m. when Callahan phoned Rob, who put his phone on speaker.

"His apartment was empty. But we got him. He was coming out of the elevator at St. Joe's, bold as day, and our officers spotted him. He had nowhere to run."

Paulie was shocked at the words that came from Rob's normally mild mouth.

"He was going back to finish her," Cheryl blurted, before succumbing to tears.

Rob took a tissue and wiped her face. "It's over now, Cher."

"Look, guys, I'm going out for a while. Don't wait up, eh?" Paulie said.

Rob frowned, but nodded. "You okay?"

"Never better," Paulie called over his shoulder as he went out the front door. The air was cool, seemed fresh and revitalizing. The car traveled smoothly east on the Ventura Freeway, with barely an effort from him.

The front doors were locked for the night, so he sneaked in through Emergency and made his way up to Kate's room. His favorite night nurse was on duty, and she smiled and turned the other way as he crept past. The officers, still present, waived him by. He sat in the chair next to her bed.

"You won't believe this, darling. Today they had a blood expert on the stand. He swears the blood on O.J.'s sock is not a spatter, but a compression stain. Can you fucking believe that? And we knew it all the time, didn't we?"

Kate lay still, her breathing steady, rhythmic.

"That bastard is so guilty. I don't know why they are wasting so much bloody time. Can you imagine if my trial had gone on so long?"

The silence in the room bothered him, so he continued to ramble. "Hey, you know that new Costner flick? *Waterworld*? Alec rather fancies the guy, I don't have much use for him.

Anyway, I heard on the radio on the way out here that it did 21 million this weekend." He paused, reflected. "You know what else I heard? That song by that guy—what's his name?—Bryan, Bryan Adams. Yeah. 'Have You Ever Really Loved a Woman?' You know me, darling, I had a right chuckle about that. Of course I thought of you, with your pink, punked-out hair."

Paulie got up, stretched, and checked the clock. It was nearly five a.m. He went to the window, peered out at the never ceasing traffic on Buena Vista. He walked around the room, then returned to his chair.

"Kate, you can wake up anytime now. The police have locked up that cursed animal. You won't ever have to worry about him again, okay? Aw, Kate, I'm so sorry, darling." He bowed his head onto her bed. "I just put it all out of my mind, I never wanted to ever think about him again. But I should have. I should have kept those thoughts, those memories within reach, else how could I protect you? I could have prevented this. He likely killed Jon, too, all because I chose to forget what he did to me. What he did to us." Tears stung his eyes and he suppressed a sob.

The touch of her hand, on the back of his head, was so light he wasn't sure if he imagined it. Paulie slowly raised up, afraid to look. She was swallowing, frowning, but her eyes were fluttering.

"Kate? Kate?"

"It hurts, Paul."

He stared at her, trying to make himself believe that she was actually talking. After a moment of confusion, he grabbed the call switch and pressed it repeatedly. The nurse rushed in.

"She's awake. She's awake! She's hurting, please, help her."

The nurse rang for the doctor on call. Paulie held Kate's hand and murmured endearments.

As she regained consciousness, she became increasingly anxious, looking quickly from side to side, clearly fearful.

"It's okay, darling. You're safe. I'm here with you, in the hospital, and you are totally safe. What's hurting, my love?"

He held her head steady in attempt to get her to focus on his face.

"My head. It hurts when I breathe. Paulie...Oh, God. It was him. David. He was at our house. He broke our picture!"

"I know. I know. Just don't think about that right now. You're safe, and he's locked up."

"Bonny! Is she okay?"

"She's just fine. She's with Rob and Cheryl."

The doctor was on the ward and quickly attended to Kate, checking her vitals and adjusting her pain medication. She was soon quiet. Paulie, however, was satisfied that she was only sleeping this time. He was tired, relieved, and thankful. He kissed the night nurse on his way out.

He put the top down on the white Beemer and cruised back to Calabasas with the pre-dawn glow at his back. He'd called Rob's cell, but hadn't roused him. He couldn't wait to tell everyone that Kate had awakened.

He called home. It was Sunday afternoon in London, and Alec answered quickly.

"Paulie. I've been worried sick, dear heart. What's going on? How's Kate?"

"She's better. She woke up! I feel good, Alec. L.A.P.D. is working with the Yard now, trying to put Stanton together with Flynn."

"Do you think Flynn is dangerous?"

"Not on his own. He's too much of a wuss. You're safe, handsome."

"When are you coming home?"

"Not sure. I need to see to Kate's recovery. You understand."

Alec sighed audibly into the phone. "Yes, Paulie. I do understand. And if I didn't adore her so much myself, I'd work hard at not understanding."

"It shouldn't be too long. And if it is, I'll just ship her back to London, Next-Day overnight."

"Not sure Rob would favor that idea much."

"Oh, yes. There's him."

Paulie turned on to Rob's roadway. "I'll chat with you later, dear. Keep the home fires burning."

"You know I will."

No one was up at the ranch, except perhaps a hand or two. Inside, the house was quiet. Paulie walked past Rob's door, then returned and tapped lightly. There was no answer. He paused, thought about his joyous news, and opened the door.

"Rob?" he said softly, peeking into the near-dark room. There was a rustle of sheets as Cheryl quickly moved to cover herself. Rob sat up.

"Oh, my. Well, fuck me. So sorry." Paulie leaned into the doorjamb. "Thought you might like to know, your girlfriend, your *other* girlfriend, woke up this morning. Cheers." He closed the door and went on to his own room, whistling softly under his breath.

It didn't take him long to stuff his scattered belongings back into his bag. He went to Bonny's room next, and packed her small suitcase, then carried both bags outside and opened the trunk on Kate's car. Rob appeared on the porch, wearing only blue jeans and a scowl.

"Look, Paul. It isn't how it looks."

Paulie dropped the luggage into the trunk, turned around. "Well, how else can it look? Lovely cliché, but it doesn't work. Cheryl's in your bed, and although she's not my type, a leggy blonde female is probably right up your alley. A naked one, at that. So I can't think you were trading recipes for shortbread."

Rob looked around, as if searching for the right words. "She's shattered by what happened with Stanton. And what happened to Kate's left us all wounded. It was just a matter of comfort, things got out of hand."

Paulie slammed the trunk lid. "Comfort. Right."

"You have no room to be self-righteous, Paul. What you did was much worse. You were married to her, for Christ's sake. I have no commitment from her. Nothing."

"Which is likely my fault, too. Kate does have commitment issues. Understandably. But my crimes don't make yours right. This, what's going on here, won't help that."

"Are you going to tell her?"

"And hurt her again? Not on your life. And honestly, I wouldn't tell her if I were you, either. But that's between you and Cheryl." Paulie leaned against the car, crossed his arms. "I love Kate. With all my being. I will forever pay for hurting her, and

I'll likely spend the rest of my life making it up to her. You need to decide what you want to do. It might take her a long time to trust anyone. You'll have to be patient."

Rob stuffed his hands into his pockets, nodded.

"And for God's sake, man, put on a bloody shirt." Paulie walked past Rob and back into the house. "I'm taking Bonny home."

Chapter 10

Monday, August 1, 1995.

Kate opened her eyes slowly, tried to look around without moving her head. She hurt all over, unable to move without a sharp pain in one place or another.

"Over here," Rob said, and she shifted her gaze further to the left, where he sat beside her bed.

"Rob."

"Right here, M'am. How're you feeling?"

"Achy. Nauseous. Thirsty."

"The nurse said you could have a bit of water. Here." He helped her take a small sip from a straw. "Better?"

"Much. Thanks." Kate slowly sank back into the pillow. "I suppose everyone knows, now, what happened."

Rob nodded, leaned closer. "I can't tell you how sorry I am for my part in this. I really had no idea that...that you were in that kind of danger, Kate. I should never have even considered letting you go back there alone."

"Neither of us knew," she said softly. "But it's over now. The nurse assured me that Bonny's okay. She is, right?"

"She's full of piss and vinegar, as usual."

"Is she with Cheryl?"

"Uh, no. She's with her dad."

"Paulie's here? Really? God. I thought it was a dream."

"No dream. He's been here since...since you disappeared. He spent the night here, last night. You spoke to him when you came out of your big sleep."

"I did? I did. I told him about the picture."

"I'm sure he'll be around soon. He was pretty tired when I saw him this morning."

A knock on the open hospital room door caused her to turn her head, resulting in pain. Two men in suits entered, one of them shook Rob's hand.

"Kate, this is Detective Tom Callahan. He's heading the investigation."

"Mrs. Bingham, I'm so sorry about your ordeal. Would you mind answering just a few questions for us?"

"No, I don't mind."

The policemen listened patiently while Kate told her story, about finding David Stanton in her bedroom, being forced into a car blindfolded and then being subjected to torture and drugs. She didn't balk at sharing the details. She saw Rob wince more than once.

"You can go out of the room if you want, Rob. I'm sorry to be so graphic, but they need to know it all."

"No. I'm okay with it."

"Now, do you believe he assaulted you sexually?"

Kate wet her lips. "In a manner, yes. He kept showing me this dildo, it was kinda bumpy, you might know the kind. He pushed it into me, yeah. I was, like, beyond caring at that point. It was after he injected me with something."

The other detective spoke up. "Were you sodomized?"

Rob rubbed a hand across his face, but Kate held her chin up. "No." She offered a sour smile. "He said I wasn't worth it. Something as wonderful as that."

"Did he disrobe, masturbate, anything like that?"

"Actually, no. All his jollies were in his head. But he did talk about Paulie a lot."

She hadn't seen him come in, but now Kate noticed her ex standing against the far wall of her room.

"What did he say about Mr. Bingham?"

"He wanted me to pretend to be Paulie. He dressed me, cut my hair, made up my face. He said things about how I had tortured Paul, kept him locked into slavery, crazy stuff like that." She smiled briefly in Paulie's direction. "I mean, how could he have known?"

Paulie chuckled. "Indeed."

Callahan closed his notebook. "That's good for now, Mrs. Bingham. Thank you for being so candid. We'll likely have more questions later. Feel better."

Paulie came forward after the detectives left the room.

"I have Bonny outside. Are you up for a visit?"

"Do I look okay? I'm not too scary?"

"Not any scarier than we look, both having been up all night." Paulie looked to Rob, whom, in turn, looked away.

"Okay, then. Bring her in. And, hello."

"Hello, darling."

When her daughter asked for the cause of Kate's "boo boos", her mother blamed them on a fall from a ladder. Rob noted that they'd all fallen from time to time, and Paulie agreed. Bonny squeezed in beside Kate, carefully arranging her tubes and wires.

"When do you think I can go home?" Kate asked of no one in particular.

"We'll have to ask the doc when he comes round. Hopefully, today," Paulie said.

"You're welcome to stay at the ranch while you recuperate. Sarah has taken quite a liking to Bonny."

"I'm taking her home. I'll see to her care." Paulie's eyes challenged Rob to argue with his plan, but Rob shrugged.

"Whatever you think is best. I thought you'd be wanting to get back to London."

"All in good time."

"Maybe you should ask Kate what she wants." Rob crossed his arms, squared his stance.

"You want to go home, don't you, darling?"

☞ For some reason, they hadn't told me yet that I'd been shot full of smack. When I did hear, the irony was not lost on me. As I laid there that morning, listening to Paulie and Rob assert themselves across my hospital bed, I felt sick. For the first time in I don't remember how long, all I wanted was my mother. And yes, I did want to go home, to my own bed, despite the fact that David Stanton had violated that space just a few days before. I could live with that, because a few mindless minutes on a Thursday afternoon could not

possibly erase the six years I'd spent in that room, with and without Paulie.

Something felt wrong about going to the ranch, anyway. As much as I cared for Rob, the thought of him hovering over me was rankling. I wasn't comfortable with him as nurturer. I promised myself I'd analyze that later.

Neither of them knew what I'd gone through with Stanton. And truth be told, I was more hate-filled, more furious than I was hurt or traumatized. Until he'd drugged me, I'd managed to keep calm enough—aside from spitting into his face and delivering a high kick to his balls. I'm sure I made it worse on myself. He hated me beyond the worst kind of loathing. Partly, just because I was female, and mostly, because Paulie loved me and not him. I taunted him, even when the barbs were biting into my ankles and my wrists, describing for him how I could light Paulie up with just a touch in the right place. The more impaired I became, the more I delighted in detailing the things Paul did to me behind closed doors. He hit me, once or twice, screaming at me to shut up, before finally injecting me again. He paused to explain that I would die, and Paulie would never see me again. It wasn't until then that I became truly scared.

Leaving Bonny motherless and with a part time father was horrifying, and I suddenly wanted to beg for my life. It was too late, however, because I must have blacked out then. The policemen said Stanton left me for dead.

Rob was quite subdued when he came to see me. He was reluctant to explain that Stanton was one and the same as Cheryl's "Stan", the elusive boyfriend she met at the gym. I couldn't begin to know what to say to her. She's had such a rough time lately. But then, we all had.

Paulie, I know, is hell-bent on taking care of me, and I guess that's all right. He is like my old chenille bathrobe. He is my hot chocolate on a cold morning, my vintage Katharine Hepburn movie on a Saturday afternoon. When he wants to be, he is my lighthouse in a storm. Now that Alec was taking care of him, he had room to take care of me.

He's an enigma.

Her release papers came through the following day. Rob, still in what Kate decided was a funk, kissed her goodbye and mumbled something about calling her later. When he'd gone, Paulie sat down on her bed.

"Mum brought you some clothes. The Staffordshire School for Boys uniform you were wearing just isn't suitable for a homecoming, now is it?"

Kate smiled, shook her head. "I'm afraid to look at myself. I have a little boy cut," she complained, running a hand over her close-cropped hair.

"I think it's rather sexy," he said. "Look. A surprise."

He'd taken to carrying a black leather shoulder bag, which he now reached into. He withdrew a small plastic hinged box, opened it. "My turn to tell you to hold still."

He painted her eyes, expertly drawing a thin line, brushing on a bit of iridescent green shadow and then applying a thin coating of mascara on her lashes. He gently pulled the bandage off her forehead and replaced it with a much smaller one, given to him by one of his fan club nurses.

"Now. A little color on those luscious lips."

Kate couldn't hold back a giggle. "I can't believe you're doing this."

"I've determined there is no way out of this place without falling prey to the hounds and flashes. You'll want to look nice on the September covers."

She looked back at him in surprise. "They'll think we're back together," she murmured.

"Do we care what they think? Have we ever cared?" he asked, but she knew he was well aware that she'd always cared too much what the public saw in the tabloids, despite his indifference.

"There. Gorgeous."

"Where's my mother?"

"She and Pop are already at the house. She's cooking up some dinners for us."

"Oh." Kate thought about her mother's take-charge attitude, her ways of dealing with adversities and challenges. Her father never had to worry about a thing because Evelyn was always there and handling it all.

Paulie helped her get into the clothes Evelyn had left, while Bonny sat on the chair and clapped her hands at every success. A sleeve, a cuff. A zipper, a button. Kate didn't remember about the sprained ankle until she stood, but the pain in her ribs was upfront and personal all the time.

A nurse arrived with a wheelchair.

"Just like Auntie Marta's!" Bonnie squealed with delight. "Can we keep it?"

Hospital security helped get them to the car, but not before dozens of photos had been snapped of the three of them. Memories of times past brought a pang of melancholy to Kate's heart.

She stole glances at Paulie as he drove them home. He was a carefree driver, a little sloppy, safe enough. When they exited the freeway, she tapped him on the arm.

"Dairy Queen. I want a vanilla shake."

"You're joking."

"No. Please. I need one."

He made a quick, illegal U-turn and accelerated back the other way down Sunset, weaving through traffic until he came to a fast-food drive-thru. "This okay?"

"It'll do."

He bought her and Bonny each one, handing them over with a frown.

"Do you know what kind of crap is in that stuff?" he complained as Kate sipped. She merely smiled back at him. Defeated by her smug face, he beckoned. "Okay. Give me a taste."

He sucked on her straw, shook his head. "Jesus. I can feel my teeth rotting."

They continued on back to the house, pausing as the newly installed electronic gates swung wide to admit them.

"Why do you stare at me while I'm driving? It's not easy, you know, switching back left side, right side, left side, right side, it's enough to send a man right off his rails."

Kate sat in her seat, sipping the shake, still belted in. "Does it feel funny, to you? Us, being here, just like this..."

"Funny, ha-ha, or funny, weird?"

"Just...like a flash back in time. Like except for Bonny being bigger, this day could be last summer instead of now."

Paulie stared at the steering wheel for a moment. "Are you rewinding, Kate?"

"Don't you ever wish you could? Would you, Paul?"

"I think about that a lot. Sure."

"To where? To before we met? Would you change things if you could?"

He turned to face her. "I think, if you could actually rewind, you wouldn't be able to change things." He thought for a moment. "Yes. I would rewind to the day we met. So that I could live it all over again."

"Even as it was?"

He nodded. "Absolutely. But I guess if you're going to talk about things that can't happen anyway, you might as well say, yes, I would change things the second time. Maybe I would take a different road one day when I'm, say, seven. Maybe I'd miss a beating by my dad, or have a better teacher, or something else that would change my path. Maybe I wouldn't be gay." He swallowed, turned around to check on Bonny, whom he'd clearly forgotten was in the car. "How's the shake, Bon?"

She gave him a toothy, ivory-foamed grin, and Paulie turned back to Kate. "I would definitely rearrange some things, obviously. Maybe Jon would be alive. Maybe my mum would be alive. I dunno. But it's like on that television program about the future, where people do make changes and then other bad things happen. Like instead of Jon, someone else would die. Instead of being, well, the way I am, maybe I'd be straight but have a voice like a turkey vulture. A *fat* turkey vulture. Who knows."

"A fat turkey vulture?" Kate giggled, then leaned halfway across the console toward him.

"What?"

She puckered her lips. Paulie sighed, obliged her with a kiss. And another. He was never one to turn down a snog session.

Neither noticed that Evelyn had come out the front door until she walked up to Kate's side of the car and tapped on the window.

"I thought you two were divorced," she complained, but her eyes were sympathetic.

Kate looked into her lap.

"Mummy likes kisses!" Bonny explained, climbing out of her car seat, shake in hand.

Paulie got out of the car and came around to help Kate. She hobbled on her sore ankle, held her breath against the bruised ribs. Paulie handled her carefully, maneuvering her to the living room couch.

"It was an experiment, Mom," she said. "I was time-traveling."

"Oh, I've done that. Many times," Evelyn said. "I hear it's bad for your heart."

Kate didn't miss her mother's double-entendre. She was right, as usual. While it felt good in the moment, kissing Paulie had done her no good. She sucked hard on her straw, hoping to annoy everyone in the room with the sound.

Her father sat down beside her while Paulie went back to get her bag from the car. Pop patted her gently on the arm.

"How are things between you and Rob?" he asked quietly.

"I don't know, Daddy. I'm sorta stuck. I don't know what I want, you know?"

"He certainly dotes on you."

"Doting might not be what I need, though."

"I understand." His eyes moved to watch Paulie as he lifted Bonny into his arms and carried her upstairs. "I'm sorry things didn't work out for you and Paul."

"Yeah. Me, too." Kate was surprised by her father's sentiment, and she carefully tilted her head to lean against his shoulder. "The good thing is, we're still close, we still care about each other, and he's a wonderful daddy to Bon."

"He certainly is. I don't think I ever told you this, Kate, but as shocked as I was when you brought him home, I was that much impressed with him as well. I knew he was queer, but that didn't stop him from loving you."

"When did you know he was queer?"

"The moment he walked into the room."

"Weren't you just stereotyping him because of the makeup?"

"He wasn't wearing any, or not that I could see. No, it was just a way he has about him."

"He doesn't exactly walk with a lisp, Daddy."

"That's not what I meant. Never mind. It doesn't matter now anyway."

Kate squeezed her father's hand. "It matters to me that you care. It matters to him, too. He loves you both, really."

"Is he still living with that other man?"

"Alec? Yes."

"Is he happy?"

"He seems to be."

"Well, okay."

Chapter 11

Tuesday, August 2, 1995. Brentwood, CA

At dinnertime, Kate called Cheryl. "You should be here. Mom made lasagna."

"I think I'll just hang out here for a while. Rob could use some company. I think he's a little put-off by Paulie staying with you."

Taken aback by her comment, Kate stiffened. "I'm sorry he feels that way."

"How are you doing?"

"Fair, I guess. Mom's mothering me, Paul's smothering me, and Pop's watching *Jeopardy*. Bonny needs a bath. I feel like bees are living in my head."

"Well...take it easy. I'll be home later, probably."

Probably? Cheryl's tone confused Kate; maybe it was just a side effect of the anguish Cheryl felt over Stanton's betrayal.

Her mother had "thrown together" a two layer chocolate cake to celebrate Kate's homecoming. Kate indulged herself with a big slab, complete with fudge filling.

Paulie clucked his tongue. "Now, you know, you can always tell a lady by the way that she eats in front o' folks like a bird! And you, here, eatin' like a field hand and gobblin' like a hog."

Kate stuck out her tongue. "I'm not Scarlett O'Hara, even if you fancy yourself to be my Mammy."

"She did have a rather chic red petticoat." Paulie raised his eyebrows and Kate forgot all about Cheryl's melancholy words. He picked up her plate before she'd eaten half of the cake. "That's enough, wouldn't want to pop another rib, would you?"

"You put that right back down, Paul Bingham," Evelyn demanded. "If she wants cake, she gets cake."

"Well, just excuse me all to...to Zanzibar."

Bonny clapped her hands, then deliberately smeared chocolate frosting on both her cheeks.

"Look, Daddy, I'm a wog!"

Paulie's eyes opened wide, and he turned away, hiding a laugh. He went to Bonny and pulled her out of her highchair. "Good grief, chile. You be needin' a bath now!" He carried her away, muttering something about washing her mouth out with soap.

It was all just too happy. Too sweet. Too much like a real family, like it was before. Kate pushed her plate away.

"Mom, that was luscious. I'm going to get a shower and just watch some T.V. in bed. Do you mind?" Kate got slowly to her feet.

"Of course not, honey. You need your rest. The doctor said—"

"Yeah, yeah, I know."

"Do you need help going up the stairs? Pop, help her."

Kate leaned on her father, and he got her into her bedroom. They could hear the bath water running, and Bonny's frequent peals of laughter.

"I remember giving you baths at that age," Pop said, giving her head a quick stroke. "Your hair was longer then, as I recall."

"Thanks. A tennis ball has longer hair than I do, now."

He smiled. "You're still beautiful. Are you safe to get into that shower by yourself?"

"I'm fine. It's just a bruised rib and a sore ankle. I'll survive. Thanks, Daddy."

He left her then, and she began the painful process of stripping off her clothes, unwinding the Ace bandage on her foot. It was worse than putting them on, when she had Paulie's help. The effects of the heroin were not entirely gone, either. A wave of pain washed through Kate's brain if she moved too fast.

She finally managed to get into the shower. The hot water felt glorious, soothing, and full of healing power. She washed her hair, noting that it only took a dime-sized portion of shampoo. It made her laugh, which made her hurt, which made her groan.

Suddenly, she'd had enough. Shutting the water off, she pulled her towel off the rack and began to dry off, taking care not to bend too much. Remember to breathe, the doctor had warned. *If it hurts, take more medication.*

Her legs would just have to stay damp. As she brushed her teeth, she thought she heard something, music maybe, or the television. She rinsed, then stood quietly.

It was Paulie singing. Not just humming or softly murmuring snatches, but actually singing out loud, his exaggerated falsetto a joy to her ears. How long had it been since she'd actually heard him croon?

"I'm hiding my tears..." he sang, covering a much loved Smokey Robinson tune.

Kate struggled into her bathrobe and opened the door.

"...throughout all these years... Oooh, oooh..." Paulie danced Bonny around the room, her sleepy head on his shoulder. He brightened when Kate appeared. "Oh, Mummy! We wanted to say goodnight."

Kate went to them, gave Bonny a kiss. Her daughter smiled.

"I'm glad you're home, Mummy. Does your boo boo still hurt?"

"Hardly at all, Sweet Bee. See you in the morning."

Paulie took her away, and Kate gingerly, painfully, pulled on a pair of panties and an old pink t-shirt. The prescription bottle was on the dresser; she placed a pill on her tongue, grimaced at the taste before gulping the water her father had brought. She slipped into bed and picked up the remote, practically panting from the effort.

She watched with interest as Paulie came back into the room and went into the bathroom, then came right back out.

"Do you mind if I use your shower?"

It was a ludicrous question, she thought. "Leave five bucks by the door."

He continued to sing, in the shower. Kate closed her eyes, listening, singing along in her mind. And when he came out, wrapped in a towel, he went straight to his bureau and rummaged for a pair of briefs. Then he got into bed with her.

"Do you mind if I use your bed?"

She took his hand. "You're messing with me."

"Things have gone awry since I left, haven't they?" He slid over so that they were lying shoulder to shoulder. She turned off the television and they were in near darkness.

"Was Rob worried about me while I was...gone?"

"Worried? He was a train wreck." Paulie sighed. "I sort of slathered him in guilt when I arrived."

"He seems really distant. And Cheryl said he was, what did she say? *Put out*."

"About?"

"You. Being here."

"What does the slacker expect me to do? He obviously wasn't doing the job."

"It wasn't his fault that I came back here alone. It was just one of those quick decisions that we make all the time. I was impatient, and I didn't know those people out there very well, the ones that were living there. I didn't want to leave Bonny with them, and I didn't want to bring her back here."

"Understood."

"And I could have gone out to his place tonight, he would have taken good care of me, he can hover as well as the best of them."

"And you didn't, because?"

"Because."

Paulie turned onto his side, and she felt his nose close to her cheek.

"Because?"

"Because I know you'll leave soon and I wanted to spend this time with you."

He laid his arm low across her abdomen, tucking his fingers around her.

"I will stay as long as you need me."

"You couldn't possibly stay that long."

He didn't respond. Kate, nonetheless, relished the feel of him beside her. He was no Superman, no Navy Seal, no doctorate-holding professor. He wasn't muscular, or athletic, or even particularly wise. But he made her feel safe. And he made her smile.

"Is it my turn to be the man? Again?"

She turned toward him, bit her lip in pain. He was offering, for once, to help straighten her out.

"Because I can do that. I can't go back, knowing that you're so unsettled."

"Is that what I am? Unsettled?"

"It seems so."

"And you? Are you settled?"

His hands were never idle, moving around her side, her back, gently stroking. "Do you remember what you said to me, that first time, a hundred years ago? I do, because it haunts me to this day. I didn't want you to go, and you said you couldn't stay. And you said to me, 'you can't have it both ways, Paulie.' Do you remember?"

Kate nodded slowly.

"When we were on top, when things couldn't get any better, I got cocky. I guess I forgot about that warning."

"That's all history, now. I need to know if you and Alec are...set in stone."

"No one is ever set in stone, darling."

She touched his cheek, pushed a short strand of hair behind his ear. "Straight answer, Paul."

"Straight answer. All right. He's thinking we should, you know, become committed. More committed."

"What does that mean?"

"He wants to get married."

Her physical reaction astonished even herself, as she felt her pulse quicken and her lungs fill with air, which of course pained her. "Can you even *do* that?"

"Sure. There are places."

"Do you...do you want to do that?" Her voice came out high and juvenile, but she couldn't take it back. She waited.

"Sometimes yes, other times, not so sure. There's something to be said for never having to worry about your partner, but then, sometimes that means all of squat, too. Case in point, Paul Bingham, failed monogamist."

She didn't argue. She felt weak, and despair began to creep into her heart. But the ibuprofen was taking effect. She took a tentative, deep breath and sat up. As carefully as she could, she crossed her arms and grasped the hem of her t-shirt, then pulled it up and over her head, tossing it onto the floor.

"What the hell are you doing?"

"It *is* your turn to be the man."

"No, Kate."

"Because of Alec?"

"No, silly girl. Because I could hurt you."

"Be gentle, but be the man. Please."

"Why? Why now?"

"Because it's my wish, the wish I couldn't tell you on the phone, and I may be twisted and off-kilter and unsettled, but if you...if you commit to Alec, we won't have another chance."

Paulie chuckled, pulled her hand away from where it crept down toward his crotch. "Okay. I'm the man, tonight. I'm your man. And as the man, I'm telling you no."

Kate pulled away. "Fuck you, then." He laughed more, tried to hold her to his chest.

"Listen to me. Listen! Will you stop thrashing about? I swear...so much for being the man. It's certainly not all it's cracked up to be."

Eventually, she lay still. Seething, and unsure why. He spooned around her, kissed her shoulder.

"I'm pretty pathetic, aren't I?" she murmured.

"Pathetic," he agreed.

"It's the heroin."

"Indeed."

"You aren't really worried about hurting me."

"No. I'm not."

"Then why?"

"I'm gay."

She again rolled over to face him, pressed against him.

"Liar," she hissed.

"It's been over a year. I've forgotten how."

"I can remind you."

"Don't be desperate. It doesn't become you."

Kate pressed her mouth hard against his, knowing the lips, the tongue, and the slight unevenness of his lower teeth. She *was*, suddenly, desperate, and the more he fought her the more she wanted from him. He accepted her kiss, let her probe his mouth, suck on his lower lip. She waited, her breath hot and rapid against his chin.

He pressed a finger to her lips.

Kate swallowed, rolled back onto her pillow. "Oh, God." *He doesn't want me.* It was bound to happen, eventually. He preferred men, had made it perfectly clear. He had a man at home waiting for him. A man that had just offered to take care of him the rest of his life, without the burden of children, or menstrual cycles, or jealous boyfriends. And here she was, still as needy, possibly needier, than the night so long ago when she'd pulled the same stunt. She swallowed again, hoping to stifle a possible sob, then she threw back the blankets and stumbled out of bed and retrieved her t-shirt from the floor.

Paulie was quick to crawl to the edge of the bed and grasp her arm.

"Not so fast. Come back to bed."

"It's okay. I get it."

"No, you don't get it. Come."

The neediness forced her to comply. He pulled her back close against him, dragged the covers up to her shoulder.

"Will you talk to me, Kate?"

She shrugged. "Whatever."

"It's important."

"Sure."

"Put aside being pissed off for a moment."

She nodded, let herself pout. It was dark, and he wouldn't see.

"What's going on with you and Rob? Honestly, now."

She wanted to turn her back, tell him it was none of his business.

"I don't know."

"Well now that's really sad."

"I told you. On the phone."

"What I heard was you backing away from a future with him."

"I'm not ready to shack up. I appreciate that he's ready, he wants to know that I'm in, but I'm not really that confident."

"Do you love him?"

"Loving someone isn't enough." She felt his chin against her forehead. "All I can think is, what if it doesn't work out?"

His hand moved to the back of her head. "Seems to me you said that before. To me."

"And look what happened!"

"Ah. I see. Maybe that's where we need to start."

"Start what? Don't be my therapist, Paulie."

"No therapy, just talk. And just so I understand, you're inferring that we failed, is that it?"

"Well, we did."

He adjusted his position, moved a leg over hers so that they were touching all the way down. The intimacy of the move was not lost on her.

"Are you comfortable?" he asked, lips close to her ear.

"Of course I am."

"Do you still love me?"

Kate looked up, hoping she could see his eyes in the darkness. They were expectant, but confident. "You know I do."

"And I, you. Are you glad that we had a child, or would you not if you could do it over?"

"Glad? She is the light of my life. I can't imagine life without her."

"Good. Me too. Now, tell me again how you think we failed so badly?"

Kate sighed. "You're playing with me."

"I wish. No. I just want you to understand that we didn't fail. We...we evolved. Yeah, marriage didn't work quite right. So we changed that. But look at us. We're still here, even when we're apart. We still fight, we still care, and we still lust after one another. And I honestly can't think there will ever be a time when we won't."

"Sure. With you married to Alec."

"Irrelevant."

"I don't think so."

"Are you jealous of Alec?"

She tried not to, but a sigh escaped. He'd waved the honesty flag. "Yes. I think I am."

"That rather tickles."

"Are you jealous of Rob?"

"Yes. Surprisingly so."

"Then why the hell are you trying to talk me into staying with him? Oh. I get it. You need to alleviate your guilt. Marry me off to Rob so that you'll feel justified in committing to Alec."

Paulie giggled, then allowed it to become a laugh. "I assume," he began, between gasps, "that you know how ridiculous you sound."

She normally would have joined in, but she wasn't quite finished pouting. And when his laughter finally subsided, he lifted her chin with his fingers and peered into her face.

"I don't want you to be with Rob, unless you want to be with Rob. And Alec or no Alec, I will always be here for you. Nothing can or will ever change that. For God's sake, at least understand that."

"How will I know if Rob's right, Paul? Dr. Creach asked me if I could see Rob in my dreams about the future. I can't. I don't see him." She stopped short of saying whom she did see.

"Maybe...maybe you need to find out if...if you'd miss him. Like, I do miss Alec when we're not together. I look forward to seeing him, most of the time, when he comes home."

"I do look forward to seeing Rob. Except lately. Just before, you know, what happened, I was kind of avoiding him. He bought us tickets to Hawaii. Cheryl said she thought he was going to propose. It scared the hell out of me, Paul. I didn't want him to ask me, because I was afraid I'd have to say no. I hate treating him like that. He's—he's a wonderful guy. He's really, really good to me. We get along great, we have lots in common, and he's just smitten with Bonny."

"You forgot to mention straight. Hey, I admit to hoping for the best, because I doubt you'll likely find another guy who will put up with me as well as he does."

Kate did smile, now. "He likes you a lot."

"He must, he shared some very fine weed with me."

"When was this?"

"Oh oh. Ganja police."

"When?"

"While you were on your extended date with David."

"I should smack you for that. Not funny."

"Sorry, darling. Truly."

"So you smoked pot with Rob?"

"Crime of the century. It wasn't the first time. But that's not what we're talking about. Listen, I need to get the rest of my stuff out of this room. I can't believe I didn't take it before."

"Don't worry about it."

"Seriously. Don't you think that's a little...intimidating to someone like Rob?"

"He doesn't sleep here. I told you."

"And you wonder why?"

"He doesn't even know your stuff is here."

"You could be wrong about that. Look, I love having mementos around, too, but I don't hang your panties around my room where Alec can see them."

"My panties?"

"Figuratively speaking, my love. I might wear them, but I don't wave them in his face."

"You may be skinny, but you couldn't wiggle into my panties if you tried."

"A few minutes ago you were begging me to."

"Now I'm depressed. All this talk is...no fun."

"Here's a thought. Go to New York."

"I hate New York."

"You loved it when we were there."

"*We. We* were there. Me there alone, ugh."

"How long is the job?"

"Four months, maybe."

"That's nothing! You should go, darling. You'll love it."

"But Bonny—"

"I'll keep her."

"Four months without her? I don't think so."

"Then I'll bring her to New York on holiday. We'll have a merry time. She'd love the Empire State Building, the Twin Towers, that gaudy statue in the harbor..."

Kate considered, reluctant to imagine herself alone and free in New York City. "Maybe."

"I think it's a marvelous idea."

"What do I tell Rob?"

"Nothing but the truth. And maybe you'll find yourself thinking about him while you're there, 3,000 miles away from him. If he cares, he'll wait."

"Maybe," she repeated.

"So." Paulie lifted his head, moved in to nuzzle her neck. Kissed the sweet spot below her ear. "I got my wish. And I didn't even have to be part of a heart transplant. So you should get your wish."

She wrapped her arms loosely around his neck, looked up as he hovered above her face.

"I'm the man. Tonight. Your man. At your service."

He showed her, now, with great care, just how ludicrous her ranting had been. He'd been right, after all—desperation was not flattering on her.

Kate opened her eyes, stared at the man sleeping beside her. She took a snapshot in her mind, wanted to forever remember how he looked, how she felt. Such uncertain times, and she thought it doubtful that she'd ever wake up beside him again.

He was beautiful, in a juvenile sort of way. She wanted to touch him, to stroke his smooth, naked back. Outline the shape of his lips, still so bruised from their marathon kissing during the night. Paulie had made good on his promise to be her man.

His hand lay on the pillow between them. She stared in awe at the tiny letters circling his wrist, intertwined with small leaves of ivy. K-A-T-R-I-N-A. Her heart swelled.

"Morning light is not kind to me," he uttered, eyes still closed. "So don't look too close."

She wanted to tell him he was always beautiful in her eyes, but didn't want to seem cloying. Instead, she urged him closer, until his head lay upon her breast. He kissed her nipple.

"Do we have to get up?" he asked.

"Not as far as I'm concerned."

"Good. I could lie here for an eternity."

"Okay. Let's."

Eternity ended in just over three minutes, when their daughter burst through the door and catapulted herself onto the bed.

"Wake up!" Bonny crawled to the side of the bed and sat up. "Mummy! Where is your jammies?"

Paulie sighed, gently tugged the covers up. "We are *so* busted."

❦ *She thought I was doing it for her, but I was also doing it for myself. She renewed me as much as I renewed her. We both enjoy sex, and each other, so much. I like to think of it as lustful devotion, what we have. I'd had nothing but gay sex for the last thirteen, fourteen months, and I wondered how having hetero intercourse would affect me. Yeah, I actually do obsess about inane things like that.*

I wonder if Kate would be offended if I said that having sex with her was like, how do they say it? Like riding a bike, no pun intended there. Something you think you might forget, but then when you get going, it's like second nature. Why do they say second? First nature. She and I, she once called us magnets. Pretty close. Snap together, hard to disengage.

We made love all night. There was a small degree of desperation, on both our parts. For all my brave words, I knew I would be leaving within a few days. I knew it would break both our hearts all over again. I did miss Alec, but never the same way I missed her.

I hated to admit it, but I'd been forced to grow up a bit. More so in the last year than in most of my adult life. The murder, the trial, the jail time. Losing the baby, even though I was informed late, was very tough. But losing Kate was the end of the world as I knew it.

I often wondered how things would be, like she said, if different decisions had been made here and there. But I meant what I said about doing it all over again. We were, still, I believed, on a grand lifetime adventure together. She had me questioning now whether I should go ahead and become attached to Alec in some ceremonial way.

Alec is a gorgeous, thoughtful, man, much sexier, too, than he appears to others. It amused me, in my looned-out head, that I might be considered-in certain circles-his wife, when I still thought of myself as Kate's erstwhile husband. Only in "My Gay World-the soap opera life of one Paulie Bingham."

Would she be all right in New York? She was nervous, but I did my best to assure her. We agreed that Bonny would accompany her, so that our little mascot could see where her mother would be living and talking to her on the phone. Then I would fly in and collect her. I'll bring Alec with me; I can't risk another heartbreaking night of intimacy with her, which would likely occur, as we are both unreasonably spineless.

And Rob? I was almost tempted to tell her about the tryst with Cheryl. But a swift mental slap reminded me that I'd not only told Rob I wouldn't, but that I'd be selling out Cher as well. And that wouldn't do. I didn't blame her for their indiscretion. She'd moved pretty seamlessly into the sister role, worlds apart from my own sister Peg, and I loved how she loved and cared for Kate in my absence.

If it weren't for my feelings for Kate, I wouldn't have thought twice about what Rob did. But I was already sensitised by what I did to her first. The fact that he did it, too, hurt that part of me that belonged to her. I know it was unintentional. I know he loves Kate. And I know that those things do happen. Obviously. –Paulie

Chapter 12

Friday, August 5, 1995

Kate drew her knees up, leaned back against the headboard as she watched Paulie drop items into his open suitcase on the bed. Still in her pajamas. Paulie focused on packing, alternately disappearing into the bathroom and the closet, pulling clothing from the bureau as well. Kate felt her lower lip jut out on its own.

As if by radar, Paulie sensed her disquiet and stopped in the middle of the room. Still wearing only a pair of nylon Nike athletic pants, his small gold crucifix swung briefly across his bare chest.

"What?"

"Nothing."

He folded the jacket he held and carefully placed it on top of the already full suitcase, then sat down on the bed.

"I know. I lied. You should know better than to believe me by now."

Kate shrugged. "You didn't lie. You placated. I knew you'd go sooner or later."

The task of packing momentarily forgotten, Paulie gently pulled the small bandage from her forehead. On the nightstand was a plastic tray containing medical supplies. He pawed through it, found a tear-open wipe and dabbed at her tiny stitches, then redressed the wound.

"C'mon. Let's see," he beckoned, lifting the hem of her t-shirt, exposing the now-yellowing purple smear across her ribs.

"It's okay."

Paulie grimaced, but leaned down and kissed the fading bruise just below her left breast.

"Now. We need to wrap your ankle."

"No. Leave it alone. Please. I'm fine."

"Stop being so surly. Haven't I earned the right to care for you by now?"

She didn't want to smile, but was unable to keep her pout going. "You just don't want to feel guilty leaving."

"Spot on. It's all about guilt. Good call."

Kate lowered her chin, but Paulie cupped it with his hand. "You tear at my heart when you do that."

"Good."

"I lay open and bleeding at your feet."

Kate stared at Paulie, wondering how long she should let him suffer. He was asking, as usual, for her acceptance. Always conditional. Love me, but let me go. I'll be around.

She slid her arms around his neck.

"You'll come to New York? Promise?"

"If you still accept promises from me, I do."

She sighed against his neck, felt him shudder in response. "Okay. Go."

He kissed her on the nose, then pulled away. She knew she'd made a monumental mistake in letting him sleep with her for three nights. It wasn't just the lovemaking of the first night; it was the comfort of his arms the following nights, when they'd whispered in the dark, relived memories and had carefully avoided the future. If he'd thought her unsettled before, he would likely be astounded to know just what a disaster she was now. But he didn't go there unless forced. And it would serve no purpose to tell him. It was a disaster only she could fix, on her own.

Evelyn and Pop left on Sunday, but not until after Kate and her mother had engaged in a heart-to-heart.

"Please don't chastise me, Mom. Maybe I don't know what I'm doing. But I will figure it out, okay?"

"Can I just tell you what I think? Look, Kate, I know we haven't always seen eye-to-eye. But believe it or not, I've been through some horribly miserable times myself. I've lived through them, and somehow I've survived. Maybe one day you'll be ready to hear about them. I know that time is not now."

"I'll get through this, too." Kate tried to smile, failed. "I'm your daughter, right? I'm stronger than you think. I got myself into this mess. I'll get out."

"You know Pop and I both love Paul. He's a loving, caring person. You and he, well, you get each other. But he's not your shining knight. He'll never be that man you need. You can't blame him for that, either, or keep hoping he'll change. It's horribly unfair to keep engaging him."

Kate felt her face grow hot with regret—and anger. Her mother was right, and Kate hated that she was. She couldn't think of how to respond. Everything that came to mind was wrong.

"I know," she said simply. "I know. It's just that...after what happened, I was weak. He was here to take care of me, to love me. I wasn't strong enough to say no."

"Rob would have taken care of you. He loves you, too."

Kate tried to swallow the growing lump in her throat. "I know," she managed to repeat.

"He's solid. Secure. You two are great together. I don't understand why—"

"Look, Mom, I don't understand it either, okay? That's why I'm going away. I have to straighten some things out. Don't make me out the bad guy here. I do care for Rob. I do. I'm just not ready to jump into something big, and if I do that and I'm not ready, everyone will get hurt. Including Bonny. I can't afford to drag her through my messy affairs."

Evelyn nodded, then put her arms around her daughter. "I do understand that. I once had a little girl, too. And I worried."

"But you and Daddy never went through the stuff Paul and I have. Things were different for you."

Her mother responded by stroking Kate's head as her daughter rested her cheek against Evelyn's shoulder. "As I said, someday we'll talk about some things. For now, maybe you're right. This trip will do you good. Just don't rule out a future with Rob. Trust me on this one."

"I'm having dinner with him tomorrow night."

"I know. He called me and Pop this morning to say goodbye."

Kate pulled back, stared at Evelyn.

"He's a thoughtful, considerate young man. He comes from the heart. And even if things don't work out between you two, I'll always care for him." Evelyn swiped at the corner of her eye. "Now, I'd better get your father moving or we'll be late for our flight."

∾ **Mom's words niggled at me for a long while. She hinted at something, some kind of discord between her and Pop. In 30-some years, I'd never seen them fight, other than the normal day-to-day domestic squabbles any couple had. The possibility of my parents having a marital dysfunction was more than I could allow at the time, so I carefully wrapped that information up and tucked it away, below my hangnail, my near-naked scalp, below Rob, below Paulie, below even my growing depression. Maybe it would dissolve under the weight.**

Kate couldn't remember if it was she or Rob who'd suggested they meet at Antonio's for dinner. There was a quiet booth in the back, and he seated her, kissed her cheek before sitting across from her.

"When do you leave?" he asked. Before she could answer, a waiter appeared and lit the candle at their table. The flickering light added an unappreciated air of romance.

"I leave this Friday. The 12th."

"And Bonny's going with you?"

"Yeah. Just for a week or so. Then Paul will come and take her back to London."

Rob nodded, took a sip of red wine. "You okay with that?"

"I guess it's a necessary evil. I can't find fault with the way he cares for her. She's excited about going."

"She'll miss you a lot."

"I know. But he'll keep her distracted."

"I've no doubt about that."

Kate lifted her wine glass, took a bigger gulp than she'd planned, nearly choked. She pressed a napkin to her lips, smiled.

"You feeling okay? Still hurting?"

"I'm a lot better. I'll be sore for a while, but I'm okay to travel and work. Thanks."

"I still can't believe you're going."

Kate looked away. "Me either. But...it's just something I have to do. I need to get away for a while."

She could see he was struggling, too. Holding back. Unsuccessful, he took her hand. "Is there anything I can do? Or not do?"

Brave smile. "Please don't think this is about you. I mean, it isn't not about you, either. It's just...I'm in full tilt, Rob. I've, like, lost my way. And I can't see the ground in front of me much less a month or even a week ahead."

She thought he might let go, but his hand stayed warm around hers.

He nodded. "I get that. Did you and Paul part on good terms?"

Kate huffed out a small, amused breath. "There are never any terms, really, good or bad. He put a Band-Aid on my face and went home to Alec. And I don't mean to...to diminish his caring. He did take care of me all week. And I'm sorry if he was a bastard to you. I can't control that. He reminds me, numerous times, that you and he are friends, separate from me. So if you have a beef with the way he treated you, then—"

"I have no beef with Paul. He has rights. Rights you give him."

"So, your beef is with me?"

Rob withdrew his hand, picked up his glass, looked at the wine as it swirled. "No. No beef. But I miss you. More than I think you want to know...or acknowledge."

She didn't know how to take his words. There was a tinge of annoyance, something she'd never heard before, coming from his lips. Not knowing how to respond, she didn't. He changed the subject while they ate.

"So the tour starts in two weeks. We kick off in Florida."

"It's finally here. You've been working on that album so long, and now you're going on the road."

"We're getting great reviews. I'm proud of it. Some of the best stuff I've ever written."

Kate smiled. She forgot, for a moment, that she wasn't allowing herself to feel good. His joy warmed her, if only fleetingly.

She passed on dessert and he raised his eyebrows. "Now I'm worried."

"Don't be. I'm really tired of people worrying about me."

Rob grew serious, his hazel eyes delving. "Kate, there are a couple of things I have to get off my chest before you go flying off. I'm sorry if you don't want to hear them, but I have no choice. Right now, my peace of mind is more important and maybe, just maybe, what I have to say will have a bearing on yours."

Suddenly fearful, Kate felt her stomach roll. Who was this man? From the depths, her instincts surfaced, those self-preserving, streetwise strengths she hadn't called upon in years.

"Okay, shoot."

Rob took a deep breath, dumped the rest of his wine into his mouth, swallowed. "This isn't easy for me to say, so bear with me." He paused, formulated. "I think you know how I feel about you. I don't want to rehash that at the moment. But while you were laying there at Saint Joe's, I nearly came apart. It was surreal, Paul was here; we hung out with Cheryl. We were all torn up, scared, keeping up the good face for Bonny, but inside we didn't know if you'd even wake up again. Then we found out about Stanton. Paul—man, I thought he would self-destruct. Cheryl just went to pieces. I never saw such suffering. She's usually so...so strong. Knowing about that other dickhead she dated, the abortion, and now this insidious bastard who'd used her in the worst way—her pain was just all over the place.

"And Paul, Paul had taken ownership of the woman I'd come to think was almost mine. Out of the blue, he broke ranks and went off to be with you, again."

Kate listened, reserved, her Plexiglas wall carefully in place. She sensed a shoe was about to drop.

"Cheryl and I polished off a bottle or two of cab. We talked, she cried. Unbearable pain. And then, then we...we ended up in my bedroom." He swallowed, looked into Kate's eyes. "We had sex. It was all about pain and comfort. Pity, remorse."

Kate felt her face color, wished she could stop it. "Really."

"I was sick with regret. She felt awful, too. It was embarrassing, after."

"I guess it would be."

"Don't blame Cheryl. She wasn't anywhere close to guilty. She was violated and trampled, and I couldn't let that go. She needed rescuing. I just didn't mean it to go as far as it did. And I'm sorry. I wish it hadn't happened."

Kate nodded. She wet her lips, looked around the red gingham tablecloth as if the words she needed would be found there.

"Aren't you going to say anything?"

"I don't know what to say, Rob. I guess I can say, I don't hold you responsible for something like that. I can say, thank you for taking care of her when she needed it so badly. I...I can see how it could happen."

Rob huffed out a sigh, signaled the waiter. "Another bottle of Sterling cabernet, please."

"You said you had a couple of things to say," Kate ventured.

"You're really not upset, are you? That I slept with your cousin, your best girlfriend, while you lay in a hospital bed across town?"

"You didn't do it to hurt me."

"I don't know if I like or hate that you are so damned understanding."

Kate shrugged. "Sorry. There it is."

He waited until he had a fresh glass of wine in front of him. Kate had never seen him drink so much before, and refilled her own glass in preparation for what was clearly still to come.

"Before I get too deep into this, I want you to know that you mean everything to me, Kate. I still believe that you and I could have something big. But there is a load of crap standing in the way, and I can't remove that crap by myself. So since you're taking a self-imposed sabbatical, maybe you'll be working on that. I hope so."

Kate tilted her head. "We'll see."

"I don't know how to put this delicately, so I won't even try. You know I care about Paul. We've been friends since, well, you know I met him before he tried to off himself on drugs. We were both young, twenty-one, maybe? And hot on the trail. We met here in L.A., at a club, he was riding high on the first wave of fame, and I was playing the small venues, trying to break in. He hit on me. I laughed it off. I was nervous, though, I'd never had a dude make a pass at me before. He bought me a drink and put me at ease, said something about me being too pretty not to be gay. He explained that not all straight boys were as straight as they thought, but he wanted to be friends anyway." Rob shook his head at the memory, and Kate found herself wishing she could have been there.

"We lost touch. You know the rest. I took some shit from my friends for defending 'the little British fag', they called him. But dammit, I never imagined that a woman would come between us."

"It's not like that."

"Like hell it isn't."

"You've always said you understood."

"My shortcoming."

"But you did."

"I wanted to. And I thought it would have gone away by now. I thought it was cool that we could all be friends. I never wanted to think that I had anything to do with your break up."

"You didn't."

"No, because you never really broke up. That's what I can't get. Let's face it—you and Paul had a weird relationship. So who was I to say that you couldn't just continue some kind of weird friendship, and move on with others? But I was wrong. You are just as dependent upon him, and he on you, as when you were married. There's no room for me in that space. Maybe you're not having sex, or maybe you are, but nothing else has changed."

"No, you're wrong."

"Am I? I don't think so, Kate. This is—this is tough for me. Last Christmas, before all the shit hit the fan with Paul and Beale, I saw a glimpse of what we could have. We were happy. You seemed to be letting all that past go. I completely understood why you had to go to London, and I supported that. I supported you, and him, through it all."

"You were wonderful."

"But then, after the trial, that night at the hotel, something happened. Something changed. You and I, we were together going into that party. You went into his bedroom, and came out his woman all over again."

"That's not true! I—I was just upset, we were drunk, and—"

"I tried to ignore it at first. But you moved away from me. Yeah, I know, I was pushing you, probably too hard. But I was scared. I wanted to rein you in. Then when you, when you were taken, I was even more terrified. I blamed myself. Paul blamed me, too, which only heaped fuel onto this already massively burning crash. He stepped right in and...and you welcomed him. No thought to Alec. Or...me."

Kate's eyes stung, the truth prompting unshed tears. She couldn't meet Rob's hurtful gaze.

He drew in a breath, ran a hand through his hair.

"So. I didn't mean to twist that into a plea for pity. What I want to say is, I hope this trip, this change of scenery clears the air for you. I know you're confused. I know it's hard for you, too. But you have to make some decisions, babe. If it's not me, so be it, but get on with your life." Rob touched her cheek, intercepted a tear.

She didn't care if other patrons saw her crying. His words challenged her in a way that she didn't want to feel.

Rob walked her to her car, in the small, dimly-lit lot behind the restaurant.

"Should I drive you home?"

"No. I can drive, but thanks."

A sense of awkwardness enveloped Kate. She wanted to kiss him goodbye, but felt like such a fraud. She opened her car door, tossed in her purse. She could tell there were more words waiting to be said, as Rob took a step away and then turned back to her.

"Look. If you want to go back to Paul, I'll have to accept that, even though it would hurt to see you make such a big mistake. A massive mistake."

Kate bristled, gave the car door a shove and it slammed shut. The earth had just tilted the other way.

"Not that I plan to, but how can you say that? I could understand if it was just jealousy, but you say that like I'm some kind of fool. How could you possibly know what's right for me?"

"Kate, c'mon. You know what I'm talking about."

"Not really, no. If you had any idea of what things are like—"

"I know you've been through a lot. But—"

"Yes I have. I've been through mountains of misery. I've been betrayed so many times now I feel like it's commonplace. Brent, Ray, and Paul, of course...I've had a baby when I never intended to. I lost a precious baby because of my own stupidity! I've lost a husband, one I thought I'd be with forever. I've been assaulted, drugged and left to die. I've learned that love just doesn't 'fix" anything, and it doesn't mean that everything's gonna be all right. I have figured out that the only person I can trust is me, and that's not even a good proposition right now."

Kate knew she was burning Rob with her eyes, but she couldn't stop.

"Are you finished?"

"No. I'm not finished. As long as I'm spewing and you're confessing, I might as well tell you that I slept with Paul. Once. When I came home from the hospital. And like you, I'm sorry I did it. Because it solved nothing."

"What were you hoping to solve?"

"I don't know."

"Then how could you know if it was solved?"

"I would have felt something besides emptiness."

"Emptiness because?"

"Because it didn't mean anything different than if we had just hugged each other. Because it doesn't fill that empty place inside of me."

"You should have been with me. You should have come home with me," Rob asserted, pointing at her in anger. "I am all about filling that empty place!"

Kate narrowed her eyes. "Can't you see? Can't you see how scared I am? It terrifies me to think I might misstep. That I might give away the farm, again, and plummet into a sinkhole."

"Is that what you think I am? A damned sinkhole? Jesus, Kate, I thought we had more than this. I really thought."

"It's easy for you. You haven't been with anyone, really, for a long time. I'm coming from a catastrophe. I've never had what you probably think of as a normal relationship. Even Cheryl pointed out that my only experiences have been with gay men and abusers." Kate placed her hand over her eyes, took a breath. "I'm even starting to wonder about my own father now."

"What are you talking about?"

"Never mind." Weary of her tirade, Kate sank back against her car. She wasn't making sense, and had to remove herself from the drama she'd created. "I'm—I'm sorry, Rob. Believe me, I am not worth all this grief. I won't blame you if you want to walk."

"But I don't want to walk. Please get that. I'm willing to resume this, hell, I'm willing to pursue you all over again. I will meet you halfway; I'll change my life for you. I've even committed to sharing you with Paul on some level. But what I will not do—" Rob cut himself off, stepped away, stared down the alley. "What I can't do is be second to him. If we end up trying to do this, I will be your partner, your lover, your man. I will be whatever you want me to be. And Paulie will be our forever friend, and we, together, will take care of him when he fails, which he will. But I will be your first, and you will be mine. If. If we do this." He returned, stood before her. "And I want, badly, to do this."

Words like "first" and "second" confused her. His assumption about Paulie's failure bothered her. The only thing that comforted was his apparent willingness to wait.

Speechless, helpless, Kate stared up at him.

Rob sighed, lowered his voice. "I'm not going to bug you while you're gone. I'll be kept busy with the tour. But it doesn't mean I won't be thinking about you every day. That I won't be hoping you'll be thinking about me. Something's gotta shake out of this whole mess." He ran his hands up and down her arms. "Do you hate me for what I said?"

"Hate you? I could never hate you, Robbie. Never."

"Did I make any sense?"

She nodded, looked away.

"You understand why I had to tell you. I couldn't let you leave not knowing how I feel."

"I understand."

"I'm not a fighter, Kate. And even if I was, it wouldn't be fair to fight with Paulie, because he's even less a fighter than I am." He embraced her now, held her tightly against his chest. "But what I am is strong. If I think there's a chance for us, I can be as tenacious as the next guy. I meant it when I said I can be what you want. I can be what you need." He kissed her cheek, let his lips linger. "Be safe. You know how to reach me."

She didn't remember driving home. Her next fully conscious thought was while trying to read the label on the bottle of sleeping pills.

Chapter 13

Wednesday, October 12, 1995. London

Alec folded The Daily Mirror and stood, swallowed the last of his coffee. "So what's on your agenda, today, Paulie?"

"Not much. I'll work on the song some more. Bonny's going with Peg to a show."

"Would you mind seeing to my dress shirts? Call to have them picked up? And while you're at it, please have that char come back. She didn't clean the shower to my satisfaction." Alec tugged on his suit coat.

"Yes, dear," Paulie mocked, giving Alec a peck on the cheek. "Don't work too hard."

Paulie muttered to himself after Alec left the house, irritated about the shirts and the shower. "He acts as if *I'm* the bloody charwoman around here." He picked up the coffee cup and plates from the table and dropped them into the kitchen sink. The cup and one of the plates shattered. Paulie turned his back on the sink, leaned against it, crossed his arms. Bonny came racing in.

"Daddy! I heard a big crash!"

"It was nothing, darling. I just put some things into the sink." He lifted her into his arms.

"Your hairs are long like mine," she said, pulling at the fine, wavy strands.

"Uncle Alec likes my hair long. But I can put it into a queue if you'd like." He put his daughter down and found the elastic band he'd put into his pocket earlier. "Like this?"

"Much better. Auntie Peg is taking us to the movies!"

"I know! What a treat! You remember what I told you?"

"Yes. Don't talk to reporters, don't show them my face. Stay with Auntie Peg."

"Correct, sweetheart."

When they'd gone, Paulie made the requisite phone calls and then went upstairs. He stripped off the kimono and sweatpants and changed into a pair of blue jeans and a dark, long sleeved shirt – nearly identical to one he'd seen Rob wear during the summer. He sat down at his dressing table, critical of his reflection. Found the last of the makeup removal wipes Kate had left him, and carefully dabbed away all traces of eye liner and foundation.

"God, I'm frightful," he murmured. *But I look male. At least.*

He found his old round sunglasses and left the house on foot. It had been ages since he'd had a good walk. Blocks passed, corners, signals, people, some recognizing him. A cop stared him down as he crossed Piccadilly. He hopped onto a city bus and off again near Covent Garden. Moments later, he found himself knocking on Meg Talbot's door.

"Paulie! Good lord! Come in, love!"

"I hope it's not a bad time," Paulie said, looking around the flat anxiously.

"No, not at all. Shannon and I were just remarking how dull it is today. And then you walked in! Can you believe it? Tea?"

"Sure. Yeah."

"Splendid. Did you drive?"

"No. Bus. I didn't think you'd be home. Don't either of you work?"

Shannon laughed. "Wish it were so, Paul. We just happen to be between jobs at the moment. I model, and Meg's an artist. Well, you already know that. Unfortunately, cash flow is rather unpredictable."

"I could see where it would be," Paulie said. "You're not starving?"

"Oh, God no. We're fine. Here; sugar?"

"Please. Two."

Paulie sat between them on the sofa as they chatted.

"So, how are things going? How's Bonny adjusting?"

Paulie smiled. "She keeps me on the sidewalk. Somebody brought us a copy of *Jenny Lives with Eric and Martin* and she shows it to everyone."

"Even Margaret Thatcher?"

"Maggie won't come round now that Bonny has an "Abolish Clause 28" sticker on her tricycle."

The girls roared with laughter.

"And with Alec? Are you blissful?" Shannon asked.

Paulie shrugged, and Meg turned her head. "I'm picking up a bad vibe. What's goin' on round there?"

"I dunno. Things are a bit close. He's a creature of habit, I suppose, and I'm more, more like the Mad Hatter. I like things that change. He likes things that are..." Paulie looked up and away, finding a word. "Excruciatingly mundane."

The two women exchanged looks. "He's only bent one way, yeah?" Meg asked.

"Well, yes, I suppose you could put it that way."

"While you, if I recall correctly, you swing."

Paulie blushed, took a gulp of tea.

"I'm sorry, love. Didn't mean to make you uneasy. We're very open people, in our house. I hope you feel comfortable with that."

"Oh, right, of course. No worries. I don't know if that word, 'swing', is quite right. I've been called 'bi' for some time. But it was only Kate. You know."

"No. I don't know. But I do know, I'm bi, and I know what that means to me. It means that sometimes I can be a woman and other times, well...I'm excited by women. Is...that...kind of how you feel?" Meg asked gently.

Paulie suddenly wanted to bolt. Meg, with her long, golden curls, low-cut blouse and shorts, was sitting cross-legged, facing him. She touched his throat, dragged her finger down to his first button.

"Sometimes it feels good to be someone else. If only for a little while."

Paulie put down his teacup. "Christ, Meg, you're my cousin."

She opened the button, moved down to the next. She leaned over, pressed her lips to his, tasted his mouth. "Two sugars. We're not starting a family, Paulie. Just having fun. Would a little pot help?"

He'd never turn down a good spliff. She lit it, passed it to him, and he to Shannon. It was gone in no time. Meg took him by the wrist, stood up.

"Today's one of those days when I feel like being with a man."

Paulie let her pull him up, glanced at Shannon.

"Oh, don't worry about her. She gets off watching. Or, helping, if you're into three's."

"Sorry, no, not into threes. I once did two—men, though—oh, Christ. I didn't just say that."

"Paulie, you are just too sweet for words." She led him to the bedroom, pushed him down onto the bed and fell down beside him. She undressed him, encouraged him to help undress her. She was all hands and mouth, and Paulie was launched into sexual oblivion. Only he didn't see Meg, exactly. Despite her height, her coloring, her voice, he thought of Kate. Remembered the moves, the things she'd taught him about seducing a woman.

The marijuana did help. Unleashed feelings, sensations he'd tucked away. Meg urged him on, rolling with him, trying different positions and touches and angles. She became aggressive, and Paulie rolled her onto her back, pinned her with his hands, drove into her when she begged. The release was explosive, painfully erotic and completely satisfying.

In the end, he fell away, stunned at his behavior. Meg was a fit of giggles, and Shannon smiled on them from the chair in the corner of the bedroom.

"Not sure you're bi, eh?" Meg managed between laughs. "I can't believe Kate let you go. You are an animal, Paul Bingham."

Paulie sat up, stared at his hands, as if they'd betrayed him somehow.

"Kate and I did it like that for six years."

"So what was the problem, baby?" Shannon asked lazily. "I mean, most would say that was good lovin'."

"I cheated on her. With a man."

Meg also sat up, pulled her blouse back over her head. "So you married a man, and now you've cheated on him with a woman."

Paulie look up, stared at Meg. "I have, at that. Haven't I?"

"But you feel good, don't you? Feel better?"

"I feel like crap. I should go. I need to clean up."

"No. Shower here. He'll never have to know. Paul." Meg grasped his arm, stayed his exit. "Stop it. It's okay, what happened here. I'm sorry if you feel like I made you do something you shouldn't. But you needed it. Didn't you?"

"I don't know what I need anymore. I'm a freak of nature. No one is right for me, and I'm right for no one."

Meg wrapped her arms around him. "That's not true," she whispered. "If you're a freak, than I'm one too, and I don't take kindly to being labeled as such. You *can* carve out a life from all this. Remember, Paulie, sexuality is a continuum; very few people are actually completely gay or completely straight....you just aren't quite as homosexual as you thought you were."

"Do you think I came here today to get laid?"

"Maybe."

"This is crazy. I would never have expected you, my cousin, a lesbian, and me...no, I couldn't have expected that. I came here because I wanted to visit."

"You don't dress like that for Alec."

Paulie glanced down at the Levi's and the Rob shirt on the floor. Alec would have lifted his eyebrows, and Paulie would have ground his teeth.

"You're right."

"What are you going to do?" Shannon asked, handing Meg a towel. "Can you live with that from him?"

"How do you two handle it?"

Meg looked to Shannon and smiled. "We fight. We bitch. We go out with others sometimes, but we always end up back here. Together."

"That didn't work for Kate and me. It won't work for Alec, either. I'm doomed."

"No, you're not. Now, look. Shannon's starting the shower. You go on, you'll feel better."

A half hour later, they were again sitting in the living room, drinking tea. Paulie turned to Meg, apologetic.

"I said the wrong thing before. It was...incredible. Thank you, love. Thanks for restoring my faith in my man-self. I do feel better. You've no idea what a complete and utter wreck I am at heart."

"You don't deserve to be. No one deserves to be lonely and isolated because of the way they feel about love and sex. You are welcome here, anytime. For tea, or conversation, or sex. Any way you want it."

Paulie stood up. "And that has to be just about the most bizarre offer ever made. But I appreciate it."

He took a wrong bus and ended up near Paddington Station. It was half-past six when he walked through the door at Chanticleer. Alec was microwaving a single-serving lasagna.

"Dear God, where have you been? I was so worried."

"Sorry, dear. I went off to see Meg and Shannon. We had tea, and I took the scenic route home. Got lost. You know me."

Alec was, indeed, eyeing the blue denim trousers.

"And I suppose your cell was dead?"

Paulie turned away, always fearful of being caught in a lie. "Hang on, I need to hit the loo."

He considered changing, but was just ornery enough not to. He rejoined Alec instead.

"So how are those wicked girls?"

"In good form. Out of work, but they have tea so all's well." Paulie peered into the freezer in search of dinner.

"I see. Sorry, I supposed you'd eaten. Oh, you missed a call from Kate."

"Oh? Did you speak to her?"

"Yes. I told her you were out, likely partying with your friends. She said it was nothing important. She'll talk to you later this week."

"Oh." Paulie closed the freezer door. Alec's tone was flippant, a punishment for the lateness, the man clothes. "You really told her I was partying?"

"Well, you were, in a manner, weren't you?"

Paulie selected a bottle of Guinness from the refrigerator. He paused at the door, turned back to Alec. "Yes. We smoked a fat wad of wacky-bacci, then had mad, gratuitous, hetero-sex."

Alec chuckled, rolled his eyes as Paulie left the room.

❧ *I was more relaxed. As the night wore on, I was quite proud of myself. I read Bonny a story at bedtime, one of her favorites about a nuclear family with a little girl, and the mother has another baby. She was long asleep when I joined Alec in the bedroom.*

"I had a client tell me today that I look like Hugh Grant," he said. "I was quite flattered."

"I had a rent boy tell me I'm a ringer for Liz Hurley," I said. He didn't care for my little joke, but he wanted sex and so humoured me with a chuckle. I made a big show of stripping off my man-clothes in front of him.

We snogged for a bit. But when he made moves to dominate, I pulled away, gave him a hard look. He turned a surprised face my way.

"You're not suggesting...?" he asked.

"Suit yourself. I'm tired," I said, and I turned my back.

He barely spoke to me the next day, didn't approach me the next night. I was about to give in on Friday when he offered to adjust our roles. I was quite smug, at first. But later, I felt empty and even worthless. I wondered if I'd done myself a great disservice by allowing Meg to seduce me, but decided that wasn't the case. She'd boosted my morale. My problems with Alec remained, either way.

October 25, 1995. New York City.

"It's another block to FAO Schwarz. Are you up to it?" Kate asked Johanna, her matronly round but ambitious girlfriend, as they trudged up 5th Avenue. "I've always wanted to buy something for Bonny there."

"What's another block? Haven't we already walked like nine blocks from Sak's?"

"Hey, this shopping trip was your idea, my friend. I would have been happy to just go to lunch."

"And that's the problem. We are living in New York and lounging and eating. We need to explore! See the city! Buy stuff!"

Kate laughed. "Of course, you're right."

Once inside, she went straight for the doll department, marveled over the high-priced designer babies and toddlers. She pointed at a sweet-faced Heidi Plusczok. "Bonny would love her."

"Yeah, just after she washes its hair in dish soap and adds Magic Marker eyeliner."

Kate considered. "Yeah. Good point. Maybe one of the play dolls would be better." She went into the next aisle, perused the rows of Götz and Beringer offerings. "Here's one with auburn curls. How sweet!"

Johanna watched her, whimsy curling her lips.

"What?" Kate asked, putting the doll box back on the shelf.

"You. You're just so different than when we first arrived. What's changed?"

"I don't know. Nothing, really."

"You were so downtrodden and, well, sad last month. You gettin' some?"

Kate lifted her eyebrows. "Are you asking me if I'm having sex? Are you kidding? And who would I be having sex with?"

A nearby shopper frowned, and Kate hurried Johanna into another part of the store.

Johanna giggled. "You crack me up."

"I do feel better. I wasn't in very good shape when I left L.A. Working has been good. I do miss Bonny, though."

"Who wouldn't miss that little sugar plum."

Kate wandered toward the stuffed animals, picked up a small lion cub. "And I miss Rob."

Now it was Johanna's eyes that widened. "What's up with that, anyway? Did you break up, or just go on ice?"

"We had some...hard words before I left. He made it clear that he was willing to wait for me to get my act together. But who knows? He's on the road. He's surrounded by hot girls all the time."

"Oh, and hot girls are what he wants? Yeah, you're right. You don't have a chance in hell, do you?"

Kate threw the lion at Johanna, who caught it with a smile. "Have you talked to him?"

"No. I think I might call him, then I chicken out. I'm not sure what to say."

"You could start with telling him how cold your frickin' bed is at night."

Kate moved on, discovered a small porcelain tea set. "Paulie bought her one of these last year." She turned back to Johanna. "It can't sound like I'm scolding him for my bed being cold. I mean, he'd be warming my bed if I wasn't such a fool."

"You're saying it's your fault you two had a falling out?"

"Mostly, yeah. Because I couldn't see him in the visions."

"So now you're seeing visions." Johanna gently touched Kate's shoulder. "Do these visions talk to you, honey?"

Kate looked quickly into Johanna's face, saw the smirk hiding there.

"Go ahead. Tease me. But I wanted to see him in my future. He just wasn't there, at first. But last night I had a dream. I was in bed, just waking, I think. I don't know where I was, but the door opened, and Bonny came in. She was with a man, holding his hand, and I was alarmed, at first. Then I sat up and I saw it was Rob she was bringing. Weird, huh?"

Johanna's eyes crinkled and she put an arm around Kate's shoulders. "I've had that dream, only the man is handcuffed, and being brought in by a cop."

Chapter 14

Thanksgiving, 1995. New York City

Kate peered into the oven, cocked her head. *It might be done. Too big to be a chicken, but definitely too small to be a turkey.*

"It was the runt of the nest," she decided, turning to the two people setting her small dinette table. "Hopefully, it tastes okay."

"It will be fine," Johanna said, patting her ample midsection. "Turkey's turkey. It's the stuffing that matters."

"Amen to that," Jack agreed. "And the green bean casserole."

"Johanna made that, so at least something will be good," Kate said. "I'm gonna take this bird out. He's gotta be cooked."

"Did you hear what happened this morning at the Macy parade? That new dragon balloon got speared on a lamppost. Big mess, broken glass and stuff." Johanna's eyes were wide.

Jack was unimpressed. "I guarantee you, ten years from now, nobody will remember who Dudley the Dragon was. They might remember being showered with glass, though."

"And they might remember getting stuck in traffic while trying to buy cranberries."

"What I heard was that four members of PETA were arrested for streaking. That's a laugh, they campaign against people skinning animals for their fur. Then they run furless themselves through the streets of New York. Sounds more like L.A. to me," Kate said, setting the turkey pan onto the sink counter. "Wish I had my electric knife."

Jack joined her on the other side of the bar separating the small living/dining area from the kitchenette. "I'll carve. It's the manly thing to do."

"Thanks. I can't be responsible for how it might come out if I do it. Yesterday I glued a bloody gash onto to Jimmy Winkee's left cheek."

"So?" Johanna asked.

"So, on Tuesday, the gash was on his right cheek. I had to work double time to catch up. It was perfect, too. Except for being on the wrong cheek."

"That's nothing. Monday I put Stella Pegg's platinum wig on upside down. She's always late, which makes me have to hurry. Then she has the nerve to complain to me that I'm slow."

Jack stabbed the turkey with a large butcher's fork. "Well I did everything exactly right this week."

"You had nothing to do this week. It would be hard to mess that up."

"True. My work was really done weeks ago. Set designers don't usually go on location. But Ted's always afraid something will change, so he drags me along."

Kate pulled a casserole out of the microwave and moved it to the table. "Well, I'm grateful that you both stayed in town. I just couldn't stomach watching Twilight Zone reruns all day by myself. Rod Serling has given me the creeps since I was little. And I am so not into football."

"No reason to go home when we'll be done in ten days or so." Johanna went to the refrigerator and found the bottle of wine Jack brought. "Too bad we're so behind schedule. Your kid still in London?"

"Yup. And they don't celebrate Thanksgiving, of course." But Paulie had talked to Bonny about the holiday, he'd assured over the phone that morning. Downplaying, of course, the need to eat a dead bird.

"Will she be home for Christmas?" Jack asked, as he layered junior-sized turkey slices onto a platter.

"No. She'll stay with Paul until after the first. It's only fair. I had her last Christmas. And she's having a blast. Nothing like two doting fathers to spoil her."

Johanna smiled. "I'm sorry, but that just sort of freaks me out. If I had kids, I think that would be hard for me."

"They're probably a lot better parents than some traditional ones," Jack muttered.

"Paulie is fiercely protective of Bonny. He keeps her away from the press, and he and Alec are pretty discreet about things. She's a very savvy little girl for almost five. I'm so proud of her." Kate perused the table, decided everything looked about right. "Let's eat."

Certainly the most bizarre Thanksgiving she'd had. Kate recalled the phone call from her mom this morning. Cheryl had flown to Albuquerque and carted her mother to Evelyn's. So at least they were together.

It was a blessing, she reconfirmed mentally, to have Johanna and Jack with her. Johanna was from Long Beach, had been doing both hair and makeup for a century, it seemed. She was generous with tips and compliments. Single, rotund, and with a kick-ass sense of humor.

Jack lived not far from Kate, in Studio City. He had those California-surfer-boy good looks, but spent his free time on the ice and not the waves. Amateur hockey and strong coffee were his vices. As misplaced quasi-Californians, the three of them bonded in the icy chill of the Big Apple.

They were just cutting into the pie when Kate's phone rang. The sound of Rob's voice caused her chest to tighten.

"Where are you?" Kate asked immediately, assuming he was in South Carolina with his family.

"I don't know. Someplace colder than a witch's tit in December. Nick! Are we in Detroit?"

"Detroit? Still on tour?"

"Yeah. I think we have about three more weeks of this grind. Are you home?"

"Naw. Still in New York."

"You're not having Thanksgiving alone?" Rob sounded alarmed.

"No. I have a couple of friends here from work. It just didn't make sense to fly out and back when we're done here in just over a week, they think."

"I won't keep you then."

Kate walked into her bedroom, pushed the door partly closed. "No. It's okay. They're just chowing down on pumpkin pie."

"Well, I didn't want the day to pass without saying hi."

"I was thinking about you, too."

"I am so ready to be done with this tour. I must be getting too old."

"It's tiring at any age," Kate said. "But worse in the cold."

"Speaking of cold, we'll be blowing through town next week. You should come."

"I heard you were doing a show here. It's in a club, right?"

"Yeah. No Shea Stadium for me. Will you be there?"

Kate smiled, imagined Rob's gentle expression. "You couldn't keep me away."

"Great. I now have a reason to continue this madness."

"If you say so."

Heater cranking away, Kate played cards with Johanna and Jack until evening, when they called it a day. Her friends had done most of the cleanup, so there was nothing much left to do. She got into bed early and cracked open a new book. She'd already spoken to her mother, her daughter, her ex and her possibly current boyfriend. Her active mind, however, made it impossible to concentrate.

Work had been good. New friends, a professional community that was so different from—and yet similar, to—the music industry. She was a highly paid, sought after artist, who'd cut a niche for herself in the world of sci-fi and horror. She wasn't just a pop star's wife; wasn't a tabloid oddity for her marriage to a gay man. Almost forgotten was the notoriety of her abduction. Despite her short physical stature, she felt taller, walked straighter, spoke with more confidence than when she'd left L.A. almost four months before.

It certainly wasn't about the money. She'd saved quite a bundle over the years, and Paulie was still sharing his wealth in a most generous way. Kate didn't bother to argue with him; she just let the money accrue, knowing that one of them would need it someday. Life was too uncertain. She recalled, with a pang, how he'd squandered everything he owned on the drug habit that had nearly killed him. This year, his legal fees must have been substantial. Fortunately, the upside of it all was the enormous spike in CD sales.

Kate closed her unread book and turned off the light. She imagined Rob, in some hotel room in Detroit. She'd never been there, but knew it was a very cold place this time of year. She was glad he'd called, and the prospect of seeing him in a week's time excited her. The memory of their last dinner together still stung, when she'd been drained of power and unable to negotiate a plan for any kind of future. Rob's offer to put their relationship on hold until she felt more capable of reconciling her life had originally made her uneasy, especially after just hearing his startling confession about an unexpected sexual encounter with Cheryl.

She hadn't blamed him. Her acceptance of the incident surprised her, and bothered her. Shouldn't she have been more jealous? Instead, she somehow understood what had happened between them. And in a way, she thought Rob compassionate in his efforts to make Cheryl feel like she mattered, that she wasn't just a rag rug that people tripped over on the kitchen floor.

He'd promised not to bug her, and hadn't. But now he'd called, and life took another turn.

⚜ **I was a little nervous about seeing Rob. I now knew that I did, in fact, miss him tremendously. Paulie had been dead-on about that, and I was grateful for his insight, for once. When he and Alec came to pick up Bonny, it was a very strange visit. Paulie was wearing a ring, a different ring, than the one I'd given him. He acted odd, at first. Aloof. Friendly, but distant. I finally cornered him on the observation deck of the Empire State building, when Alec was helping Bonny see through the viewers. Paulie was reluctant, but couldn't hold back the news that he and Alec had tied the knot at an informal gathering in the English countryside.**

I wanted to throw him off the top of the skyscraper. Not because he'd gotten married, but because he hadn't told me, hadn't given me a chance to even wish him well. I was mad that he felt unable to confide, to share the joy of the occasion. Did he really think it would be better to wait and let me find out on my own? Shame on him.

I let him see my anger. He apologized all over the place, and hugged me, but of course I pushed him away. Alec kept a distance, understanding that Paulie and I had to have it out. I knew it was a good thing, but I needed time to process it.

That night, in my dinky little apartment, the three of us talked and agreed on how their union would be described to Bonny. They both kissed me goodnight when they left for their hotel, and I wept just a little after Bonny went to sleep. But what else is new? Me, crying about Paulie, was nothing out of the ordinary.

The next day, we did a little more sightseeing. Paulie was more relaxed, more affectionate. We got Bonny a New York pizza. We took in Times Square, and saw a Rockettes show. Paulie took my hand at the end of the evening, pulled me into the bedroom of their high-priced hotel suite. He grilled me about Rob and me, again. I told him about how Rob had slept with Cheryl, and he confessed that he knew all the time. I was astounded. The fact that he hadn't told me was another betrayal, almost bigger than the act itself. He explained, tho, that he'd made a promise to Rob, so I respected him for that. He seemed to be very forgiving of Rob, and encouraged me to give Rob another chance. I told him it wasn't about chances, and that I'd never been very upset about what happened. It was just about how I felt about Rob, and giving up my independence. He didn't comment on my thoughts.

I left Bonny with them that night, with her little suitcase all packed. Paulie accompanied me home in the cab, and saw me safely inside. He didn't stay long, but we held each other in a marathon hug that I thought might never end. I told him how much I hoped things would work out with Alec, and quietly reminded him that I was always his second. He was too choked up to respond, and fled before we both ended up knee-deep in tears.

I tried not to think much about Rob. After our parting in August, I sort of convinced myself I was unworthy of him. So much of what he said was true, and the memories of my illusion-filled nights with Paul the week before slammed me into reality when I was finally alone in New York. What an unfathomable fool I'd been. But when Rob called on Thanksgiving, I was overjoyed, and couldn't wait to see him again. It was as if we'd never been apart. I decided not to fixate on those visions of the future that had plagued me in the past.

Chapter 15

December 3, 1995. New York City

Kate emerged from her bedroom and turned for Jack, her smile demure.

"Damn, woman. Let's forget about this whole sordid mess and just order in," he teased.

Kate grinned. "You tempt me, but you're too young."

"This Evans guy isn't gonna know what hit him."

Johanna bustled into the room, all rustling in holiday taffeta. Jack threw an arm around her shoulders. "I already have a date, Miss Katrina. But thanks for the offer."

"Oh, Kate, honey, that dress is a knock out. But you'd better cover up your bosom. You don't want snow falling into your cleavage."

"You don't have to worry about that. I've never had any cleavage to speak of. Do I really look okay?"

Jack and Johanna looked at each other and both laughed.

"Are you nervous, honey-bunny?" Johanna asked. "This guy will salivate all over you. And besides that, he happens to adore you as well. What could you possibly be worried about?"

"I'm more worried about Rob. He doesn't stand a chance," Jack said, shaking back his hair and pulling on his sport coat. "You women are stealth."

Kate went to Jack, corrected his collar. "Only because guys like you make us crazy."

"Hey. Hands off my date," Johanna quipped. "Here, doll face, put on your overcoat."

Jack slipped on the coat and a scarf, and went to the door.

"I'll hail you ladies a coach. It's the manly thing to do."

He was back in less than thirty seconds. "Uh, there's a limo at the curb. Seems Ms. Bingham has friends in high places."

They were escorted to a stage-side table. Jack sat between the girls, again citing his manly duties, and they were served complimentary cocktails. Kate's anticipation was over the top. Just before curtain, a red rose and a small envelope appeared before her.

"Kat, you are too beautiful for words. Unless the guy is your date, your friends are welcome backstage after the show. If he is your date, please note that I lied when I said I wasn't a fighter."

Kate smiled, looked around, wondered where Rob was watching her from.

"Dinner later, hope you're hungry. Love, Rob."

"What does it say?" Johanna whispered across the table.

"It says he's going to take Jack out."

"Whoa. Wait a minute, here. I was only joking about ordering in." Jack moved his chair closer to Johanna's.

Kate laughed, and Johanna frowned. "What are you talking about?"

"Never mind. He wants you guys to come backstage after the show."

Jack shook his head. "Naw. I don't want to embarrass the guy. Besides, Johanna and I have plans. Don't we, Jo Jo?"

Johanna started to protest when the lights went down. When Rob walked out on stage, Kate felt all the air leave her chest.

He moved up to the microphone, tuning his guitar as he walked. "Hey, New York."

The room cheered.

"What's up with this snow?" he asked, noodling a little on the strings as the crowd responded. "It's good to be back. Here's an appropriate lead off tune. 'Manhattan Christmas'."

Kate couldn't take her eyes off him as he sang, and he spent more time than not looking back at her.

Every other song seemed directed at her, songs of love, romance, hope. Jack teased her, lacing his fingers and resting his chin on them with a sigh. Johanna punched him but Kate missed the entire display as she watched Rob's hands now glide gracefully across the ivory keyboard. As much as she wanted to enjoy the show, she couldn't wait for it to be over, and soon, it was. An escort came to their table.

"Mr. Evans asked me to accompany you backstage," he said, draping her woolen winter coat over his arm. "All of you."

"Actually, we have plans," Jack said, standing up and offering his hand to Johanna. "But please tell Mr. Evans we appreciate the offer." He squeezed Kate's arm, leaned close to her ear. "Go get him, girl."

"Thanks, Jack. I'll see you two tomorrow. Thanks for coming with me."

She watched them wander out of the theater with the crowd, and then allowed the young man to show her to Rob's dressing room. She didn't have to wait long.

He stopped just inside the door, apparently taking her in as she stood with her back to the dressing table. He took a step forward, reached out to her, and she closed the gap, took his hands.

"Hi," she said, marveling at how good it felt to touch him.

"Enjoy the show?"

"Of course."

"Where are your friends? I didn't scare them off?"

"No. They...had plans. Another time."

"Hungry?"

"Starved."

"I just have a few things to—"

"No, you don't." Nick came from behind him, smiling at Kate over Rob's shoulder. "Get outta here. I'll lock up and turn out the lights. Hey, Kate."

The limo waited at the curb, and rushed them off to 44th Street for a late supper.

"You've been here for almost four months and haven't been to Sardi's?" Rob chided, as they entered the famed eatery.

"Nope. No reason for a fancy dinner. Until tonight."

Conversation was light. Kate talked about *Independence Day*, her new friends, the weather in New York. Rob shared stories of the tour, his sister's latest pregnancy, his father's hernia operation. They shared a *Boccone Dolce* for dessert. Rob seemed relaxed, easy, himself. Kate hoped she didn't appear as nervous as she felt.

"Are you sure you want to see my little closet of a home?"

"Absolutely."

"Okay. Don't say I didn't warn you."

The snow had thickened when the limo stopped in front of Kate's apartment. Kate started up the steps and Rob dismissed the driver. Once inside, she showed him all of her three rooms. When he begged off to use the bathroom, she made them hot chocolate and waited on the couch.

"You will love this. Taste!"

Rob took the hot mug, sipped. "Wow. Peppermint schnapps?"

"It's called a Snuggler."

"Yum."

Kate got up, went to the window. "You have to see this. It's the best part."

He joined her and she pulled open the drapes to reveal a stunning view of the New York skyline, already adorned with rows of twinkling holiday lights.

"Wow. Awesome. Did you have to pay extra?"

Kate only smiled.

"Hey. C'mere."

When she was within reach, he slipped his arms around her waist. "How...how's life treating you?"

"At the moment, it couldn't be better."

"Oh, I think it could be."

"How so?"

He stole a kiss, and another, then spoke into her ear. "Like that."

Kate looked up at him, tried to reconcile the man in her arms with the man on the stage. The man who'd comforted her on the plane. The man who'd quietly held her up during some of her darkest moments, who'd laughed with her and cooked for her.

"Wait," she murmured. "I might have missed that. Again?"

He smiled, showing those rarely seen dimples, the melting snow in his hair making it hang onto his forehead.

"Not sure I can duplicate exactly, but it was something like this."

This time she was ready for him, and returned the kisses in kind. They moved to the couch, kissed some more. Kate came up for air.

"Are you sure you want to do this? We haven't talked." She wanted to bite her own tongue for saying it, but something didn't feel right.

"I do want to talk. We have a lot to say to each other." Rob sat up, smoothed back his hair. "But I'll admit to hoping that actions might speak louder than words."

She smiled. "Yeah, sometimes that's true."

"You wanna go first?"

Kate pressed her lips tightly together, clasped her hands in her lap. "I guess what I want to say is, those things you told me, back in August, they were all pretty much true. It was hard to accept. When I got here, after they took Bonny, I had a sort of a meltdown. I made up my mind that I wasn't going to see you again."

"*What*?"

"I decided I wasn't, you know, right for you. I'd behaved so badly. You're a better person than I am."

"Are you nuts?"

"As it turns out, yeah. My friends, Jack and Jo Jo, they helped by pushing me hard into work. We did a lot of walking around this ugly town. And then, it wasn't so ugly anymore. We talked a lot. Jack has a girlfriend in L.A., and he's had some troubles with her, too. Johanna's been through it all. So I was just, like, healing. Paulie helped, too, even though I'm sure he didn't mean to, telling me how well things were going for him."

Rob didn't move, waited for her to continue.

"Slowly, I started to feel different. Like maybe I was going to be okay. I realized, though, that you might still be too pissed off at me, and I'd just have to live with that. Then you called."

"Not right for me," he muttered, taking her hand. He examined her fingers one by one, preparing his words. "How could you even consider making a decision like that without me? Is that what you do? Figure everything out for yourself?"

"I've been accused of that. Yes."

Rob shook his head. "No. No good."

"I might need you to cut me a little slack. Haven't you ever done that?"

"I had a meltdown, too. It might have been Chicago. I went on stage pretty boozed up, that was a first. Thank God for Nick. I wouldn't have gotten through it without him. I thought—I thought I'd blown it with you. I said some pretty harsh things. Like, it wasn't my place to judge you. I couldn't possibly know what you'd been through. When I sobered up, Nick sat with me, we sat there looking at that icy river and he said some stuff to me. About him and Sarah, and how rough it was at the beginning. Sarah was a recovering addict. She'd come from a hellhole of a family life. Dad raped her. Stuff like that. He told me that you and I, we could make it. He said I wasn't wrong to come down on you, but that I had to be patient, too. That love is never black and white, only a million shades of grey."

"Nick is smarter than he looks."

Rob grinned. "Yeah. He is."

"So?"

"So. Can we establish that we've met halfway? That we just might be right for each other? Is it worth pursuing?"

"Will there be rules?"

Rob peered into her face. "I think, yeah, relationships need some kind of boundaries. Don't you?"

Kate nodded. "Yes. I do." A vague memory passed through her mind, of a time when she agreed to lower her expectations about fidelity. "If something has enough value to be worth protecting."

"Whoa. Where'd that come from?"

She smiled. "I don't know. But I might need baby steps right now."

"Me, too. We can get to those boundaries later." He bent slightly, slipped his arm behind her knees and lifted her, carried her to her bedroom and deposited her on the bed.

He lay down beside her, stroked her cheek. "Is this okay?"

Kate nodded. She liked how he asked. She liked how he took his time, how just necking was enough. For now.

"I've never felt so connected to anyone before," he said softly. "Both physically and emotionally."

His words prompted one more kiss. Then she pulled her lips away and crawled off the side of the bed.

"I'll be right back. I need to take care of a little...housekeeping. The bed warmer is on, make yourself...comfortable."

Inside the tiny bathroom, her zipper wouldn't come down. She sighed, closed her eyes, centered. "Slow," she said silently. She tried again, this time pulling the tab all the way down. She hung up the dress, dug into her cosmetic bag for her diaphragm, took time to remember how to insert it. *Not a good time to get pregnant.* "Not at all."

A little perfume, and the cute black teddy she'd tucked under the sink *just in case.*

She was relieved to find Rob already in bed. It would have been a horrendous mistake had she misread him. He immediately pulled her close, and she ran her hands over his shoulders and down his back. She was stunned to realize that he'd lost weight—possibly fifteen pounds or more. Still muscular, but while he'd never be boyishly slender like Paulie, Rob had cinched at least a couple of belt notches. Was it because of her?

She dashed the thought and allowed herself to enjoy his efforts to remove the teddy.

The clock on the nightstand read 1 a.m., and Rob touched Kate's shoulder.

"I should go, Kat girl. I gotta be on a bus for Hoboken at ten in the morning."

"How far is your hotel?"

"I'm not sure. Twenty minutes?"

"Then just leave early. Don't go now. Don't." As if she could prevent him from going, she climbed on top of him and laid her head on his chest. He engulfed her.

"I can't tell you how much I've missed you."

"I've missed you, too."

"Will you think about something? For me?"

"Sure."

"Come back home with me for Christmas."

Kate smiled, delighting in his voice in the dark. "I don't know. My family—"

"Can come, too. Evelyn and Pop will get on great with my folks. Bring Cheryl. Bring the whole goddam family. Just come, babe."

Kate rose up, kissed him on the mouth. "I'll try."

"Will Bonny be home?"

"No. She'll be in London."

"Have they been back?"

"Not since they took her in August."

"How is Paul, really?"

Kate swallowed. She knew the topic would come around eventually. "He seems fine. He and Alec, well, they got married. In August."

Rob raised his head, then lay back down. "No shit."

"Yeah, huh? Just like that. He...he didn't tell me about it, either. The wanker."

"I can't believe you just said that." Rob chuckled. "That's a pretty offensive word."

"He deserves it."

"Yeah, I guess he does if he didn't tell you. Wow. So that's, what, four months? And they're still together?"

"Paulie's become quite domestic. I guess he likes being a wife."

"Well, duh."

It was Kate's turn to rise up. "Why do you say that?"

"Because I wouldn't think big Doc Doyle the type looking for a husband, sweetie."

Kate lay back down. "You're right. It's just hard for me; it's always been hard for me to see Paulie both ways."

"You have the unique opportunity to do so."

"I guess."

"When do you go home, again?"

"Around the 18th or 19th. You?"

"The 20th. Good timing."

She sensed he wanted to say more, but was relieved when he didn't, and soon she heard his rhythmic breathing turn to sleep.

When she next opened her eyes it was 8:30. Her back was tucked against his chest, his arm was around her waist. She turned her head.

"Robbie. Wake up. You need to go."

"Hmm?"

"Come on, lover boy, wake up,." She kissed his forehead, pushed back his hair. "Robbie, baby, remember Hoboken."

His eyes fluttered open. "Oh, crap. I'm late."

"No. Not yet. But you could just stay."

He smiled, stretched. "Wish I could. Nope, the fans are too important." He gave her a loud kiss on the ear, then got out of bed. She watched him gather his clothes and head into the bathroom.

Now, she stretched, too. She felt like Scarlett O'Hara after her infamous night with Rhett. Felt like singing. Like eating chocolate and like committing.

The thought made her laugh. Chocolate and committing?

He came back, searched the floor for his shirt, found it.

"You promise you'll think about Christmas?"

Kate sat up, pulled the blankets to her chin. "I promise. It sounds nice. I just don't know how Marta is doing. If she's still stable, maybe, but..."

"I understand." He sat on the edge of the bed, put on his shoes and socks. "But I'd hate to disappoint my momma by having to stay with you in L.A.," he said, leaning down to give her a kiss.

"Resorting to a little blackmail?"

"Whatever works."

He dashed then, leaving Kate to wonder at the change. In herself.

&#x0001; *From Rob: Cautiously optimistic. Maybe I hadn't blown it after all.*

I have to admit, I did a double-take when she walked in with the blond kid. I mean, this guy looked like MacGyver only prettier. He couldn't have been with the older gal, the one with the obviously healthy appetite.

But Kat looked like a little goddess, smiling, walking into that club like she knew right where she was, and where she was going. The guys were having my ass for peeking, but I couldn't tear my eyes away.

Later, in her postage-stamp sized apartment, I could hardly believe the change in her. Said she'd had lots of time to think about what she wanted—music to my ears, because clearly, at least that night, what she wanted was me. So much so that she did something completely out of character from the Kat I know. The lace teddy was an adventurous endeavor for a girl who's most comfortable in her oldest, softest t-shirt. Which, by the way, would have been just as enticing to my eyes as the black lace, snapped crotch and tiny red satin bow.

But her willingness to consider spending the holidays with me excited me most of all.

Chapter 16

December 19, 1995. Los Angeles, CA

Another trip home from the airport, another winter's day, Cheryl was driving. Had it really been a whole year? Only this time, Cheryl was happy, animated, listening and contributing to the conversation. Kate was almost suspicious of the happiness of the day. No horrendous news waiting at home?

Monday-afternoon-before-Christmas traffic plagued them, but neither seemed to mind.

"I love your new car. It's an Integra, right?"

"Yeah. I couldn't wait to get rid of the Ford. You know, after everything. This car is so much newer, anyway."

"It's sexy."

"Yup. So I hear."

Kate's BMW was parked in the garage. "Is it still running?"

"I start it up once a week, kiddo. No worries, there."

Inside, Cheryl brought out a feast. Salad, rolls, fruit.

"You made all this?"

"Don't get excited. It's a bribe."

Kate giggled. "Whatever for? What could you possibly want from me?"

"All in good time. You said you had something you wanted to ask, first."

"Oh. Yeah. Hmm." Kate stuffed her mouth with baby greens and feta cheese. "Mm. Yum."

"Yum and what?"

"It's about Christmas."

Cheryl looked wary. "What about it?"

Kate scrunched up her face. "Rob wants me, uh, us, all of us, to come to South Carolina. I don't think Mom and Pop would mind, but I wasn't sure about you and your mom."

"You're kidding."

"No. Not kidding."

Cheryl took a bite of salad, chewed slowly, and eventually swallowed. "Well, I don't know."

"I understand. Is Aunt Marta not doing well?"

"Oh, she's doing great. In remission, still, and feistier than ever."

"Then?"

"Well, I have this teeny tiny problem. I've been, Mom and I, we've been invited elsewhere for Christmas."

Kate paused, fork in air. "Invited elsewhere? Like, where? With whom?"

"With my new man, that's who. He's invited us to Christmas in Mammoth with his family."

"What new man? You've been dating and didn't tell me?"

Cheryl put down her fork. "Yeah. I didn't want to say anything until, well, it was more real."

"Who's this guy and when can I meet him? I don't let my best girlfriend-slash-cousin go out with just anyone, you know."

"And I can understand that, what with my less-than-stellar record for choosing guys lately. But you'll approve of this one. In fact, I think that's him," Cheryl said, getting up to answer the door.

Kate's jaw nearly dropped when Lt. Tom Callahan walked into the kitchen, holding Cheryl's hand.

"Hi Kate."

"Detective Callahan? Oh my God. Didn't I just talk to you a few weeks ago?"

"Yeah. About the trial. I'm sorry, Cheryl wouldn't let me say anything."

Kate's smile was so broad she felt her face might break. "I don't freakin' believe this. I'm—I'm shocked! But happy!" A spontaneous hug with each of them followed her exclamation.

"So you see, this might work out to our mutual advantage. No guilt!" Cheryl said.

"Rob comes home tomorrow. I can't wait to tell him."

December 23, 1995.

Rob and Kate collected her parents at Augusta Regional Airport just a half hour after they arrived from L.A. via Columbia. Evelyn and Pop were in good spirits, and Rob was happy to see his brother Glen pull up to the curb in their dad's brand new Lincoln Town Car.

"Y'all have a nice flight?" Glen asked, methodically loading suitcases into the ample trunk space.

"Yep, w'all did," Rob twanged back. "Mom ready for us?"

"You know Momma. She's hissy-fittin' around the kitchen, Shanie's hissy-fittin' around with her big ol' belly, Dougie's hidin' out in the barn, Jesse's runnin' from the mob. Bidness as use'yal."

"Now Glen-Bob, you're gonna scare off Kat's people talkin' like that," Rob teased, holding the back car door open for Evelyn.

"You couldn't scare us off if you tried," Evelyn said, reaching up to pinch Rob's cheek. "Remember who raised Katrina."

"You have a point, Eve," Rob agreed, earning a jab from Kate.

As expected, their parents got on famously from the start. Jean accommodated Evelyn's need to help in the kitchen, and Chuck was more than happy to take Pop on a tour of the property via his newest golf cart. Kate got to hear all about Shanie's challenging pregnancy while Rob caught a beer with his brothers. Bedtime came three hours earlier than it would at home, but the Newmans welcomed the guest room and turned in with everyone else.

Rob's bedroom was the only one not in the main level of the house. Built later, the small add-on included a bathroom and was located over the living room.

"How did you rank this private room?"

"I was obnoxious."

"I see."

"It's going to be cold," he warned, as they got to the top of the stairs. "I forgot to turn the heat on earlier."

He wasn't kidding, Kate decided. She sat down on the double bed and shuddered. "I think I heard the sheets crack."

"No, that was my knee. Lemme see if I have one of them thar electric-type blankets like my New York honey has on her bed." He dug into a small linen cabinet. "Nope. Stolen. I knew I should have locked the door."

He went to Kate, wrapped her in a bear hug. "Guess we'll just have to make our own heat."

"That's not cliché, is it?" she asked.

She woke early, dressed quickly, and pulled on her fur-topped boots. She kissed Rob lightly, then crept downstairs to the kitchen where her mother sat drinking coffee with Jean.

"Good morning, Moms," Kate said.

"Mornin'. Coffee, honey?" Jean asked, holding up a mug.

"I was hoping there was some left."

"Sleep well?" her mother asked with a smile.

"I think we thawed out around midnight. Tonight will be different, I guarantee you this California girl will figure out a way to warm up that room in advance."

Jean chuckled. "Robbie has an electric blanket somewhere. I think Jesse might have borrowed it."

"Rob didn't use the word borrowed to me," Kate said, adding some milk to her coffee. "But it gave us an excuse to get cozy."

"Like you two need an excuse," Evelyn said.

"True! So what are we doing today? How can I help?"

"We are making pies. Your momma and I have been tradin' recipes. I have some peaches I put up last summer just for a Christmas pie, and Eve here is tellin' me about a pee-can pie that will rot our teeth."

"Sounds yum. Are these-here pies for tonight?"

"No. We'll fix and hold 'em for tomorrow's Christmas dinner. Tonight we have a hayride, and maybe some carolin', you know, we do Christmas big around here."

"I guess so," Kate murmured, looking out the window at the snow. "How deep is it?"

"Not deep. Maybe an inch or two. We rarely get any at all, but might get more tonight."

Kate sat on a barstool, listened to her mother chat with Jean. She felt oddly at home, comfortable, even stress-free for the first time in...maybe ever. She had no place she needed to be, had two mothers at the ready to handle Christmas. Bonny, she was certain, was well-cared for and delighting in her own first snow. And the man who was just now wrapping his arms around her was the biggest reason for Kate's joy.

Evelyn poured him a cup of coffee.

"Where is everybody? Thanks, Eve."

"Pop's still snoring," Evelyn informed.

"I sent your daddy down to the market for some Crisco. Can't make a proper crust without it. Dougie and Shane are still sleepin', and Jesse hasn't shown his face yet, either."

"I'm here," the younger Evans called from the couch in the family room.

"He's hungover," Rob said. "Lightweight."

His brother returned a moan. Rob took Kate by the wrist, tugged her across the room to the coat rack, and grabbed her pink snow parka.

"Put this on, baby doll. We're going for a walk."

"Out there? In the cold?"

Rob rolled his eyes. "Get used to it. Love me, love my South Carolina." He helped her shrug into her jacket, then put on his own. "We'll be back sometime."

Kate took a last, savoring sip of coffee and let him lead her out the door. She trudged, at first, then forgot her discomfort as Rob pointed out the sights along the way. The ice on the birch trees. The small, frozen ponds here and there.

"In the meadow, we can build a snowman..." Rob sang, and Kate giggled.

"Is all this land theirs?"

"Yep. This is part of the original Winter Colony. All these big ol' properties. Ours was built in 1833, we have something like forty acres, straight back." He motioned with his hand. "My dad used to board thoroughbreds. Made lots of money. Paid off the estate. Bet a little, now and then, mostly lucky.

Bailed Glen out of his divorce and some bad investments. Bailed Jesse out, literally. Took care of Shanie while Doug was away."

"What about you?"

"Oh yeah. He's bailed me out more than once. Car payments on a 1969 Camaro that I blew up, just after I wrecked it, just after I lost my job. Talked me out of enlisting when Mary Lee Jacobs broke my heart."

"You weren't exactly the bad seed."

"We didn't always see things the same way. He thought it was stupid to run off to L.A. But he owned up proper when my first single hit number one."

"And when you got your Grammy? And your three albums went platinum?"

Rob smiled, shrugged. "I'm not sure he totally gets that, but it doesn't matter. I flew home in October when he had his surgery."

Kate clutched at his arm as they walked through the patchy snow, and again throughout the day and evening as they joined their families for song, for laughs and celebration. It was a Christmas Eve like no other, filled with snowball fights, the smell of baking pies and adoring glances from all.

After hot rum drinks around the fire, Rob stoked the small but elaborate woodstove in their bedroom and turned on the mysteriously recovered blanket. They sat facing each other on the bed, laughing about the day, excitedly anticipating Christmas morning. At midnight, he reminded her to call Bonny, who would likely be up and waiting to hear from her mother.

Bonny was spinning with delight, with tales of Santa landing on the roof at Chanticleer, about the cookies and milk she'd left, and reindeer tracks in the snow. Kate could hear Paulie's softly whispered prompts in the background.

"And thank you, Mummy, for my Felicity doll. She's beautiful, and she looks just like me!"

"You're welcome, sweetheart. Oh, how I miss you! Do you have lots of snow?"

"Everything is all white. Even Daddy's hair!" she exclaimed, falling into a fit of giggles. "Daddy says I make it white!"

Kate couldn't help but join in her daughter's laughter at Paulie's joke. She was still chuckling when he came on the line.

"Merry Christmas, darling. I hope all's well."

"It is. Everything is great. So is Bonny being a pain?"

"She is...an absolute toad!"

Kate could now hear Bonny in hysterics.

"Give her lots of hugs and kisses for me."

"I will. And for me?"

"And for you. Please give Alec my love."

"And me?"

"Of course. What did you get for Christmas?"

"Only the most gorgeous, custom-made Gaultier jumper you ever laid eyes on."

Kate smiled. "Nice."

"And you?"

"I'll have to let you know. Not Christmas here yet."

"Oh. Right. Well then, tell Rob I hope he gets everything he deserves, about which you are the judge."

"I will."

☙ I didn't really want to think about what Ev was giving Kate for Christmas. Since we are now all aware that I am more than one person, it won't sound odd when I say that 'a part of me' was quite chuffed that she was back with him. And a part of me, that snitty, snobby, tantrum-throwing she/male spectacle was blowing him a raspberry. Go ahead, take her, pull the rug right out from under me.

Truth was, I missed her. I needed, badly, to tell her what I'd done, and done again, with Meg. My cousin had become my personal concubine, but I didn't confide in Kate. We had mad, blind-folded sex, where I thought about Kate and Meg thought about—God knows who. I'd never seen Meg with a man so I couldn't visualise it.

I knew Kate would disapprove. After all, I was cheating—again. But holding the knowledge inside of me was dangerous. I didn't trust myself. I was a walking time bomb, and I feared Alec's discovery of my infidelity daily. Hourly. For a person who cannot lie, living with my crime was a new kind of hell. –Paulie, born with XYZ chromosomes.

Chapter 17

December 25, 1995. Aiken, South Carolina

"It's Christmas now, right?" Rob asked.

"I guess you could say that. It's after midnight."

"I was going to wait to give you your gift, but I'm too excited."

Kate squirmed forward, until their knees were touching as they sat on the bed. "Well then, I guess I'm excited, too."

"But I have to talk to you about some things, first."

"You're not dumping me?"

"Nope."

He took her hand, let his fingers play on the back of it. "I'm not real good at this stuff, so bear with me. Now, I know, last summer, I was...over anxious about some things. I tend to get that way. When I was a kid, my momma would purposely make me wait for things I asked for; she said she was teaching me patience."

"She wasn't exactly successful."

"I do try."

"You wanted me to move in with you. I wasn't ready, then, but—"

"I know my timing sucked. I think things have settled some, now, but I've sorta changed my mind."

Kate's lips parted in surprise. This wasn't what she wanted to hear. "How so? You don't want me as a roommate anymore?"

"Not exactly." He paused, reached for his backpack on the floor and dug inside. "You remember that old game show on TV? Where the contestant had to pick from door number one, door number two, or the box on the display floor?"

Kate laughed. "Yeah. I remember."

"Okay. You get to play. Only we're going to skip over door number one."

"Why?"

"Because you don't want what's behind that door, and neither do I."

"Is that, like, the donkey?"

"Yeah. But here we have number two, which is an envelope. And..." he again pawed through the pack, withdrew a small blue velvet box. "This is the box on the display floor."

Kate's eyes grew wide.

"You might recognize the envelope," Rob said, picking it up and waving it in front of her.

"Yep. I do." It was the same envelope he'd produced on her birthday, containing airline tickets. "But I'm really curious about the box."

"Of course you are. So here's the deal. If you choose the box, you also get the envelope, but that box comes with a few strings. Now, I remember promising you baby steps. So you can choose the envelope if you want, and I'll take back the box."

Kate frowned. "But the envelope doesn't have strings?"

"Only one. Only that you consider, that means just say that there's even the tiniest possibility, that you might opt for the box later."

"Opt for the box. Hmm." Kate reached for the box, but Rob snatched it away before she could touch it. "Can't I see it?"

"Nope. You have to decide. That's the rule. You never saw Monty Hall letting the contestant see what was behind the door!"

"What are the strings?"

"Well, that's the thing. They don't exactly meet your needs for the baby steps, you know? And I respect that. I do, Kate. But I need to tell you, I'm ready for those...strings."

Kate smiled, tilted her head. "You didn't say what they were. Even Monty Hall would tell me that before asking me to make such a difficult choice."

He was quiet, toyed with the box in his hand and then placed it on the bed. He took her hand. "Until I met you, I thought I'd been in love before. Looking back, it's no wonder I wasn't interested in falling in love again, because I'd never really experienced anything close." He lifted her hand, kissed the palm. "The box comes with a lifetime commitment, and asks for one, too. It comes with devotion, and loyalty and respect, and as many babies as you want."

Kate uttered a tiny gasp, pressed fingers to her lips. There was no ordinary dinner ring in the box.

"It's real. It's what I want. And I've never wanted anything so much in my life. But..." his voice softened, and he reached out to stroke her cheek, "it can wait for a while. Because I want you to be absolutely sure. You can take the envelope, and I won't be upset. Much."

Her fingers were shaking, ever so slightly, as she reached out, her hand hovering over the envelope. She looked up, into Rob's expectant eyes.

What am I doing? What should I do? As if burned, she quickly withdrew her hand and briefly covered her mouth.

"Can't I buy a vowel or something?" she asked, a tentative smile forming on her lips. Rob smiled back. The dimples were persuasive.

"Wrong game show. But I forgot to say one part. Maybe the most important part." Now he took both of her hands in his. "I love you, Kate. I love you, I can't live without you, and I want you to be my wife."

Kate swallowed, hard. Rob's eyes were fixed on hers, willing her to choose.

An odd sort of calm came over her. The confusion began to clear. She let go of his left hand, picked up the envelope. He drew in a breath, lifted his chin, but didn't speak.

"Love's a funny thing," she murmured. "Sometimes you can be looking for it, and it's right in front of you." Kate dropped his other hand and snapped up the ring box, pressing it, and the envelope, to her chest. "I want it all. If that's okay."

Rob cupped her head in his hands. "Are you sure? Really?"

"I'm scared. But, I love you. I do want to marry you. I want to be your wife."

He took the box from her fingers, opened it for her. "Then this is for you, babe."

Kate stared at the exquisite engagement ring, the large, octagonal diamond, the simple white gold band. "It's...it's beautiful, Robbie."

"It's an Asscher. A little over two carets. I got it in New York." He slipped it onto her finger. She panicked, for a moment, worried that it wouldn't fit, but once past her knuckle, the ring settled perfectly into the narrow space on her third finger. The finger that had felt oddly miserable since she'd wrested her old wedding ring off a year before.

"You have no idea just how happy I am," he said softly. "I'm a little scared, too. I want us to be forever, Kate. Do you think we can be?"

She looked at him, his hopeful eyes, his sincerity shining onto her. She knew his question carried extra weight, because there were special circumstances. She had a troubled ex. She had a young daughter. She had issues, herself, yet to be fully resolved. But as she stared back at him, the ring now warming to her hand, she nodded.

"We can be forever, Rob. We can."

The light went off, and with the fire crackling in the stove beside the bed, Rob made what she would always think of as Christmas love to her.

⮞ **Mom and my wonderful Mom-in-law-to-be both caught sight of the ring immediately, and my mother pulled me aside. Her joy was only slightly overshadowed by my own, and Jean positively beamed all afternoon. They promised, however, to keep my secret until Rob could announce it at dinner, which he did with a sort of charming, humble bravado.**

In the back of my mind, my darker side waited for a second shoe to drop, but it never did. Even the fleeting thought that I would have to tell Paulie didn't dim my lights. There, in the winter wonderland of Aiken, I discovered the truth about myself: that I really did want a life with Robin Evans. That elusive, murky future was suddenly illuminated by the brilliance of the diamond on my finger. Rob was there, after all, flying kites with Bonny, standing beside me when my

mother grew ill, pushing a baby stroller around Descanso Gardens.

I couldn't really tell him how he'd magically appeared, because I'd never shared my fears about his absence in the first place. But it didn't matter. On the flight to London, we were already acting like newlyweds, kissing and giggling and planning. He sang to me, prompting applause from the ten other passengers in our cabin.

And when I told him that he might have given me another, very personal gift that Christmas morning as we made love, he didn't bat an eye. Instead, he kissed my cheek and whispered —"Let's hope so."

Chapter 18

Saturday, December 30, 1995.

Although she would have preferred going home first and having time to prepare, Kate agreed with Rob that as long as they had to board another jet, they might as well pick up Bonny on the way home. Paulie was thrilled that they would be in London for the holiday. Fares were through the roof, being New Year weekend, but Rob opted to pay the extra 20% and hitch a ride on the Concorde from New York. It was Kate's first flight on the luxurious British Airways SST.

"It seems so narrow."

"It is, compared to the wide-bodies you're used to flying. But we'll be touching down at Heathrow in about three and a half hours."

"Amazing." Normally, Kate would have welcomed the shortened flight time; the almost eleven hours from L.A. wasn't something she enjoyed. But today, in light of the news she was bringing, three hours didn't seem nearly enough.

Rob squeezed her hand. "The D.A.'s office still saying April?"

Kate nodded. "Not looking forward to that. Who knows how long it will last, either."

"So...you think we should have the wedding before it starts?"

"I think that's a wonderful idea, yeah. March would be good."

"Well, the fifteenth is Bonny's birthday, right? If I remember right, it falls on a Thursday this year. We could go for the seventeenth and still have time for our trip to Hawaii."

Kate smiled. "Saint Patrick's Day. I like it. We'll all wear green."

"Kelly or forest?"

"Kelly for me, forest for you. Or olive."

"Have you thought about what kind of wedding?" he asked.

"Cheryl asked me if we were doing traditional or wacky. I told her I did wacky the first time. What about you?"

"I did Vegas the first time, which definitely qualifies as wacky."

"I know my parents would like to see me more officially married, but I'm not into churches. Maybe something else, traditional, fancy, but not church-ish?"

Rob nodded. "I like that idea. You could even wear shoes this time."

Kate looked down at her new engagement ring. It reminded her of the summer in New York, when she'd spied Paulie's new ring as they rode the elevator to the top of the Empire State Building. She didn't want him to suffer the same shock, hoped he wouldn't see the ring before she could tell him. It amused her, momentarily, to consider keeping her left hand buried in the pocket of her jacket.

She turned her attention back to Rob, belatedly absorbing his jab.

"I might wear shoes. I might even wear panties."

"You're stressing about telling Paul, aren't you?"

"Yes. I kinda am."

"He'll be happy for us."

"He will. And he won't."

"Do you want me to tell him?"

Kate turned to Rob, smiled. "It's my hope that we can tell him together. But things never go the way you want them to. More likely, I'll end up telling him alone. It'll be okay. I can handle it."

"Well, Alec, at least, will be overjoyed."

"You're probably right."

Heathrow was a zoo. Neither had the patience to wait for a cab, so Rob hired a limo to drive them out to Chanticleer. As they were getting out of the car, Rob stared up at the mansion. "You think we should have called? He was expecting us on the later flight."

Kate shrugged, hoisted her shoulder bag. "Too late now. It won't matter."

She rang the doorbell and waited; it was a big house. She was poised to ring again when the door opened and Alec invited them inside.

"Well, well! What a wonderful surprise. We weren't expecting you for at least four more hours. Come, just put those bags down and have a sit."

Kate pulled off her coat, handed it to Alec. "I'm sorry, we caught the Concorde instead. I forgot to call and warn you."

"No matter. Paulie's just taken Bonny for a walk round the street. They'll be back soon, and delighted I might say. May I get you a cup of tea?"

Rob shook his head. "Alec, you are the epitome of grace. I think you've managed to purge the last nasty bit of Americanization out of yourself."

"Ah, you Yanks aren't half bad. Tea, Kate?"

"Sure. Why not. Where did you say they went?"

"Oh, here or there, Paul needed to get out." Alec left them in the parlor, called over his shoulder, "it's been just a year today, you know."

A year?

Rob grimaced. "Good timing on our part, huh?"

It took Kate a moment to catch up, but realization dawned. "I can't believe it. A whole year." She sat down on the settee, remembered the anguish of sitting there before in shock and misery while Paulie sat in jail. Alec was already returning with her teacup.

"Yes, time flies," he said, putting the cup and saucer on the coffee table. "He's being melancholy, and it's his right, but I've been trying to distract him all day. Perhaps your presence will do the trick."

Oh, yeah. That and my wonderful news. Some distraction.

"Everything else going well?" Kate asked, taking a sip of tea. "Is Bonny okay about going home?"

Alec tilted his head, gave her an odd smile. "She's had a good time here. She's young; she doesn't quite grasp it all. She and Paulie are extremely close. I hope that doesn't bother you."

"Bother me? It delights me. The last thing I want is for them to grow apart."

"I can almost guarantee you, that will never happen."

As if cued by some celestial source, Bonny's laughter carried into the room from outside, followed by Paulie's bellow of mock commands. They chased into the room together, stopped abruptly at the sight of Rob and Kate sitting with Alec. Kate hastily stuffed her hand into her jeans pocket.

Panting and rosy, Bonny trilled her joy and leapt into her mother's lap, prompting the hidden hand to respond. Rob stood, gave Paulie a handshake and then a hug.

"Why you bleedin' rascals, turning up early like this!"

"Bleedin' rascals," Bonny repeated, slipping off of Kate and rushing Rob with her unbridled childish affection. Kate stood and embraced Paulie briefly.

"We were just having a little cuppa. Get yourself one, dear, and join us." Alec touched Paulie's shoulder.

"I'm actually quite sick of tea, Alec," Paulie complained, pulling up a chair. "So what made you so early?"

"They caught the Concorde. Isn't that just tops?" Alec said.

Paulie gave him a chilly look, then turned to Rob. "Did you just love it? I so wish they'd fly into L.A."

"It was really awesome. I'd flown it once before, but it was Kate's first time," Rob replied, holding Bonny on his lap and entertaining her with a small packet of mint candies from his shirt pocket.

"Ah, a virgin Concordess. So what did you think, darling? Isn't it just the sexiest plane ever? How was your Christmas?"

Kate laced her fingers, pushed them between her knees. "I loved the flight, and yeah, I guess you could say it was sexy." She glanced at Rob, then back to Paulie. "Christmas was fabulous. Not as much snow as you, but we had a great time."

"I'm sure you did," Paulie murmured.

The ring of the house phone interrupted an uncomfortable moment, and Alec got up to answer it in the kitchen. Bonny slipped off of Rob's lap, took his hand.

"Come and see my room, Rob Evans. Come and see my toys Santa brought me. You, too, Mummy!"

Kate looked from Bonny's face to Rob's. Rob stood up.

"I think Mommy would like to rest, but I'd love to see your new toys. Mom will come later."

Bonny dragged Rob from the room and Kate turned to Paulie.

"How are you?"

"Over thirteen stone and smoking a half pack of fags a day."

"That bad, huh?"

"It was a year today that Jon was killed."

"I know. I'm sorry. And we should have called first." She reached out, intending to touch his knee; his look stopped her, and he tilted his head just slightly in the direction of the kitchen. Alec had a clear view of them from where he sat talking on the telephone.

"No, it's quite all right." He swiped at a lock of wavy, ashen hair, swept it behind his shoulder.

"It grows really fast," Kate remarked.

"Not mine."

"Oh." She didn't like his makeup, either. Too much shadow, wrong color on his lips. Very femme, conjuring images from the days of the Boyz.

Kate frowned. "Where can we talk?" she said softly.

"Later. I'll think of something."

"No. Now."

"Are you trying to make my life more difficult?"

Kate smiled. "Let's go see Bonny's toys."

On the second floor, they could hear Bonny excitedly sharing her bounty with Rob. Paulie took Kate's hand and quickly pulled her into the bedroom she would share with Rob that night.

"Okay, Mata Hari. Make it fast."

Kate drew in a deep breath. "We will tell you both later, but I wanted to tell you myself. Alone." She reached up, placed her hands on his shoulders, and looked him in the eye. "Rob proposed. I said yes."

Paulie didn't flinch. "It's about time. Let me see the bloody ring."

She didn't show him. Instead, she pulled him down, into an intimate hug, sank against him in relief. In return, he whispered in her ear.

"You are one lucky little girl, you know that? Did you think I wouldn't be happy, Kate?"

"I wasn't sure what to think."

"I've told you many times."

"And I'm supposed to believe you?"

"Good point."

She let him hold her for a bit, until he pulled away with a nervous glance over his shoulder. "We're going to have a few people over tonight. You and Ev should get a nap in."

Kate nodded. "We still need to talk. Maybe tonight?"

Paulie hesitated, licked his lips. "Maybe," he whispered, then, "Let's go see Bonny."

"Okay." Kate followed Paulie out the door, then heard Alec's footsteps nearing the top of the stairs.

Kate and Rob did sleep, the exhaustion of celebration and travel catching up with them. They woke and dressed, then joined the others around seven o'clock. Paulie was fully engulfed in his starring role, wearing a brightly striped caftan and a freshly made up face.

Kate tugged on his sleeve.

"Where's Bonny?"

"Upstairs with Missy and Regan. You remember the girls? I've hired them to mind her for the evening. Okay with that?"

"Sure, if you are."

He introduced her and Rob to a few friends they'd not met before, then asked Kate to answer the doorbell that continued to ring.

Megan and Shannon flounced in, Meg giving Kate a lavish hug and a benign kiss on the lips.

"I don't think you've met Shannon, my girlfriend. Shan, this is Paulie's Kate."

Kate winced at the intro, but shook Shannon's hand, marveling at her flawless, coffee-with-cream complexion.

"Darling Kate. We've talked so much about you. All good, love." Shannon looked past Kate. "And you must be Rob. Glad to finally meet you."

"Same here," Rob said, accepting Shannon's hand.

They'd not yet closed the door when more guests arrived, including William Teasdale and his recently reconciled wife, Mary, along with son Kip. Kate felt joy at seeing them, and was surprised when Kip introduced a young male companion.

All totaled, there were, perhaps, thirty people in the house, including Peg. Kate was relieved to see her former sister-in-law, for whom the word "former" obviously did not exist.

"Yes, I moved the banshees from the house earlier this year. When the doctor moved in, we went out. It just wasn't right, you see, but Paulie found us a lovely little house not far away, and truth be told, we're happier. No more pounding feet up and down the stairs, worrying about waking his lordship. And," she added, lowering her voice conspiratorially, "it's better for me as I now have a gentleman caller."

Kate lifted her eyebrows and Peg giggled.

"He's a constable, not a bad thing to have in this family."

"Ha! You're joking. You're dating a cop? So is Cheryl!"

They shared a good laugh. Peg again tried to suffocate her with a hug, and Kate let her, and her joy, seep in.

Paulie tapped the side of his glass with a spoon, and Rob turned off the music.

"I have a something to say, so if you want to stay and party, you'll have to listen first."

After a general muttering from the crowd, Paulie began. "I want to acknowledge a couple of things, and we'll get the sad one out of the way first. For those of you who haven't remembered, it's one year ago tonight that our friend Jon Beale met his tragic end in Hampstead Heath."

Even the whispers stopped, and Paulie looked solemnly around the room.

"I spoke with his mum today at the cemetery. She hasn't even begun to heal, but she was kind to me. As so many of you have asked, I do want to bring you up to date. Barrister Teasdale has news I'd like him to share."

Teasdale looked up, flustered. Cleared his throat. "Well, I do, yes, I've heard some information. Apparently, our most efficient justice system has been successful in getting accused killer David Stanton extradited from America to stand trial here in Britain. This will, of course, delay the Americans from trying him on assault and kidnapping charges, but I don't think anyone, including his...his sweet and unfortunate victim, will mind." He looked directly at Kate, whose hand flew immediately to her mouth as the others cheered.

"Are you sure?" she asked, and the barrister nodded benevolently.

"We just heard today. I'm happy to be the first to tell you."

"If...if he's convicted of murder here in England, will he still stand trial in the U.S.?"

"Yes, but it would likely be a short and perfunctory event. If convicted here, he'll likely earn a life sentence. If convicted there, which he surely will be, he could receive a consecutive life sentence."

Kate had barely recovered from the news when Paulie raised his voice again.

"In other news..." he quipped, reaching for Rob's forearm and pulling him to stand beside him, "this is my good friend Robin Evans, and I believe Mr. Evans has an important announcement as well."

Rob smiled, shook his head at Paulie.

"Come on, sweet face. Don't embarrass me, now."

"Okay, yeah. I do have something." He looked across the sea of faces to Kate, where she still stood beside William and Mary Teasdale. "Uh, Kat?"

She made her way to him, gave him her left hand, which he raised into the air.

"Ladies and gents, this woman, *my* sweet and unfortunate victim, has agreed to marry me."

The loudest squeal of joy came from Peg as the crowd erupted into congratulatory laughter. It seemed everyone in the room wanted and needed to hug Kate and Rob. Alec hung back, waited until she was free, then offered his arms.

"I can't tell you how simply delighted I am, Kate. You've come so far in a year."

Kate felt awkward allowing Alec to touch her. Vibes were strong, and negative, from the time she'd walked through the door earlier in the day. She swallowed it down, kissed him on the cheek.

"Yeah. It's been an amazing journey. Rob and I are really excited."

"Quite clearly. I wish you the utmost happiness, dear. And I know Paulie does, too."

The party ended early. Alec left to take the sitters home, and Megan and Shannon were the last guests to leave. Kate could hear them call their goodbyes, and she hurried from the living room to catch them. She paused, however, before entering the foyer.

"It was a lark, love," Megan was saying, pressing her long, lean frame against Paulie's as she moved close to kiss him. Kate squinted. Even from twenty feet away, she could see that lots of tongue was involved, and her mouth dropped open as Megan grasped a handful of Paulie's posterior as she kissed him. Shannon, standing behind her shockingly lustful girlfriend, smiled.

"See you Wednesday?" Megan asked as she pulled away.

"Sure." Paulie nodded. "If I can get away."

Astounded and speechless, Kate went upstairs and got into her flannels.

Rob was watching television, but picked up the remote when she got into bed.

"Don't turn it off on my accord. I'm too wired to sleep."

"What's up? Did he tell you what's going on?"

"No. I wasn't just imagining it?"

Rob put down the remote. "It hit me in the face like a wet blanket when we walked in. And I don't think it has to do with us."

"No, I don't either." She couldn't tell him, just yet, what she had witnessed downstairs.

Rob yawned through half of a horror movie. Kate threw back the featherbed.

"I think I'll go tidy up a little in the kitchen. I'm just really antsy."

Rob gave her a look that said he understood it was not the kitchen that needed attention. "Don't stay up too late. And... let me know if I can help. Part of the deal, right?"

She nodded, but knew if she couldn't fix Paulie, no one could.

Chapter 19

Lying on the couch, Paulie peered at the dying fire, his arms wrapped around his stomach. The wig was gone, the makeup hastily removed, the gown replaced by a long sleeved t-shirt and sweats. There was an untouched snifter of brandy on the coffee table.

Kate knelt on the floor.

"Did you want to talk about Bonny starting school?"

Paulie's gaze remained on the fire. "Sure. Whatever you and Rob think is best. She needs to be challenged, else she'll grow bored."

"We might look at a charter school that's not far from the ranch."

"Sounds good. I'll trust you to know what charter means."

Kate placed her hand on his arm, quietly absorbed him. He was in crisis.

"Stomach ache?"

"Nausea. Perpetual."

"Talk to me, Paul."

He looked at her now, his eyes darting from hers and away, then back, then away.

Christ, it's worse than I thought.

"I've really nothing to tell you. Things are going well. I'll miss Bonny when she leaves. I'm thrilled to death about you and Rob. That's it." His voice was soft, uninspired.

"Is Alec asleep?"

"Likely."

"Are you really okay? Getting along with each other?"

"Why wouldn't we?"

Kate glanced at the empty staircase, listened momentarily to the sounds of the house. "Oh, I don't know. Maybe because you're shagging your own cousin?"

Paulie flinched.

She hoped he'd deny it, but he didn't speak.

"Explain this to me."

He offered up a small shrug. "I can't explain what I don't understand."

"Does he know?"

Paulie's eyes opened wide. "God no. He'd string me up by my privates if he knew."

Kate narrowed her eyes. "So I let you off easy with a slap?"

"You did more than smack me." Paulie peered into her eyes. "You scare me sometimes, Kate. You steal my thoughts. My secrets."

Kate tried to read him, but failed. He wasn't finished, so she waited.

He swallowed. "I don't know how to be anymore. You know, when I was a teen, a young teen, I guess, when I was enlightened and liberated by some guy I'd met at a club, I was overjoyed to finally understand that I wasn't alone. That there were others out there like me. That being gay wasn't some dread disease that I would have to keep hiding. I mean, sure, I got that it wasn't status quo, and my mum and dad didn't exactly share in my joy, but I no longer felt like a freak. When you came into my life, you upended my core beliefs, fragile as they were. You liberated me, too, in a far different way."

"I thought it was good."

"It was good. But..." he looked away, searched for the right direction. "I need rules that stick. I need to feel like I know myself. I don't do well when the ground moves beneath me. I thought I wanted things to be black and white. Do you understand what I'm saying?"

"Yes."

"I loved being a man for you, Kate. I did. Most of the time, it felt...absolutely perfect. You believe that, right?"

"Of course I do."

"But there were these voices. Images. Thoughts...things I couldn't control. The *she* in me was suffocating."

Kate felt as if she, herself, was suffocating, just listening to his story.

He looked back into her eyes. "I thought, with Alec, that I could be back under control. That I could dress how I want, be how I wanted, however the mood struck, you know?"

"And you can't?"

He looked away.

"He wants you to be...the she...all the time."

"He tries to be accommodating. I'm so complicated. I'm work, for anyone."

Kate ventured a smile. "I can't argue with that."

"Cheek."

"But you're hearing the voices, again. Different voices."

"It's not like I'm schitzo. No. But they, the thoughts, they pull at me. I can't be any one way, all the time." Paulie sat up, patted the couch beside him. "Come. Off the floor."

Kate joined him, sat sideways with her knees up. "He still loves you. That's clear to me."

"I never really understood this bisexual thing. Even though it *was* a convenient explanation for my sudden 180 with you. But it wasn't just any woman or all women, it was only you. So I didn't buy into it. My mates, other strictly gay men, they bitched and moaned at me. But now I'm not so sure."

He shook his head. "And I think, *I miss Kate*. I miss how we were together. The troubling times, I conveniently forget. I remember the good times, how good you were to me, how you tried to let me be all of those people. At your expense, darling. I know that. And I also know that...that Rob is absolutely right for you.

"But I lie awake at night, wondering, what the hell is love, anymore? I'm more confused than ever. Look at me! I'm thirty-five fucking years old, and I thought, well, I knew my life wouldn't be a bloody walk in the park, but I thought I'd at least be somewhat settled by now."

"You shouldn't fixate on feeling 'settled.' You're different. That doesn't make you wrong. You're just—"

"If you say I'm fucking *special* I swear I will launch you across the room." He grasped her chin, gave it a little jerk. "My mum used to say I was special. But I got that I was special like Mrs. Henderson's retarded son down the way. Special like the two-headed snake I saw at the traveling circus."

He did have two heads, inside. Kate had never seen him so clearly before. She took his hand, held it with both of hers. He added his other hand to the bundle.

"That night you came to me, explained why we had to separate, you said something to me that I've held in a death grip ever since. You said we were soul mates, Kate. I wasn't really clear what that meant, but I knew what I wanted it to mean. And when I'm feeling bad, alone, lost, it's those words that I cling to."

His voice was breaking, and she heard the anguish.

"It means exactly what you think it means. Listen to me. You can't live like this. If you're doing what I think you're doing, you are damn well gonna get caught. You need to talk to Alec before this goes any farther. Christ, Paul, he's a goddam shrink! He doesn't even know you."

"You are the only person on this earth who knows me. I get scared sometimes. Alec will never know me. No one will ever know me. Only you."

"You're afraid to let Alec know you. Don't be. You can't share true love until you share yourself. You're afraid he'll reject you."

Paulie shook his head. Kate lifted his chin.

"You don't have to share everything. Just...just enough so that you can feel you can be yourself. If wearing the apron and the pearls all the time is too much, tell him, dammit. You have needs, too. Damn if I didn't learn that the hard way. But of all people, Alec should be able to understand. If you talk to him."

"It really isn't his fault, any more than it was yours. His expectations are not unrealistic. He took me on—"

"He took you on knowing your past. He was your therapist. It isn't like you hoodwinked him into a relationship."

"You are always my cheerleader. You make *my* expectations unrealistic. It's long been known, in certain circles," he said, tugging on a lock of her hair, "that you have spoiled me."

"Be that as it may, you are screwing up royally. You need to stop this thing—whatever it is—you've got going on with Meg. You seem to always crave that which you can't have. If you want her, leave Alec. But I'd put money down that you don't want that, either."

He smiled at her. "You are so lucky, my sweet love. Look at what you've got ahead of you. Your future is clear now. I'm so happy for you."

Kate sighed, allowed a moment to pass. He wanted a response.

"Rob is my perfect man. We're going to have a wonderful life together, and hopefully have lots of babies and good times. You understand, right?"

Paulie nodded, blinked.

"He's easy, and devoted, and strong, and I love him. I hope we stay together always. But you, you and I, we are welded. Soul mates? Yeah. And I love you whether you are being a man or a boy, or Bette Midler or Alice down the rabbit hole. I love you when you are pitching a tantrum, and even when you're lusting after that cute waiter at Mario's. I love you when you are being the best father Bonny could ever have, and when you're crying over *Philadelphia*."

"But why?"

"I can't answer that. I've asked myself that question, a million times. Why you and me? Why do I know that whatever happens, you will always be there, somehow?"

Paulie sniffed, tried to smear away his tears.

Kate took the edge of her cuff and dabbed at his cheek. "I wish I understood. But I don't. So I've stopped trying. You keep hold of those words, okay?"

He was still weeping.

Kate huffed. "Cheryl will kill me for doing this," she muttered, then climbed onto his lap, pulled him close until their noses were touching. "I need you, Paulie. I need you to be strong. I need you to try and make this work with Alec. It takes effort. And no, it's no bloody walk in the park sometimes. But it's no fun wandering through life unhappy and worried and scared. You've said as much to me."

"I know."

"I need to know that you'll be there to answer the phone when I'm having my own meltdowns. Because I will have them. I'm work, too, don't forget, and Robbie will likely call you in exasperation. And Bonny is going to need your gentle hand when I'm flipped out of my mind."

He nodded.

"And likewise, in times like now, I am your go-to. My light is always on. I don't care if you are wearing an Armani tux or a pink silk frock. I don't care if you've made your face up like Leigh Bowery or if you are stripped down to bare flesh and air. Because when I look at you, I don't see any of that."

"What do you see?"

"I see the you who exists beneath it all. I see a loving, honest, unique human being, somebody that I cherish. Someone generous and caring, and preciously real. Don't ever feel you have to change. Please."

"From your lips..." he murmured.

"Now, give me some love before I go upstairs," she demanded gently.

They shared a tender, chaste kiss, and he embraced her.

"Okay." Paulie issued a shuddering sigh. "Still spoiling me. You know I will absolutely die if you ever leave me."

Kate smiled over his shoulder. "No pressure."

"None whatsoever."

She held him for a minute. Stoked his back. Felt his tension begin to dissipate. It eased her pain, just a little. He pressed his lips to her ear.

"Can I be in your wedding?" he asked, creating a shiver down her back.

"What would you like to be? Matron of honor, or flower girl?"

"I want to give you away."

"But...Pop is supposed to do that."

"He already gave you away. To me. It's only right for me to give you to Rob."

Kate pulled back, looked into his face. "You make that sound incredibly sad."

"I know. I'm good at that."

"I need to go to bed," she whispered.

He ran a hand through her hair, let his fingers slip down to the shiny ends.

"I can't go up there yet."

Kate stood, walked to the base of the back stairs. "You want to sleep with us?"

"I do, sort of."

"You're sick, you know that?"

Paulie nodded, picked up the brandy. Kate climbed the stairs slowly, every step a challenge. She found Alec waiting outside her bedroom door.

"Is he going to be okay?"

She peered up at him in the darkness. "I'm not sure."

"Is it something I can fix?" he asked softly, his voice tinged with fear.

"I don't think so." She touched his arm lightly. "But try to. Please. Try."

Moments later, she climbed into bed and laid her head on Rob's shoulder. She was thankful when he didn't ask.

☞ From Rob: I knew without her saying a word that Paul was a mess. She was weak, as if she'd given all her strength to him by transfusion. It saddened me. She'd worried all the way to Britain about telling him, hoping against hope that he'd be happy for her. For us. Something had gotten in the way.

But the next morning, miraculously, they were both fine. Paul was upbeat and even jovial. Kate was full of spunk and good cheer. Only Alec seemed more reserved than usual, but I certainly wasn't going to ask why.

Bonny's joy was infectious, as well. Although I didn't expect her to, Kate sat down and explained, in terms a precocious five year old could understand, that our family was changing again and would be even more wonderful than ever. She surprised even me, when she asked Paul and me to sit together while she identified Paul as Dad #1 and me as Dad #2. Bonny further delighted us all by suggesting that Paul was her British father and I, her American one. She sealed it by climbing onto both of us at once, demanding a group hug. Despite the childlike spontaneity, Paul's embrace was warm and sincere. I'll never forget it.

We took Bonny home amid tears and promises and anticipation for seeing Paul and Alec at the wedding. Paul was hesitant to let us go, but I could see Kate's strength had restored him. At least for now.

She never did tell me what transpired between them that night. I knew it wouldn't be the last time she would be called upon to comfort him. It was something we would always live with. I accepted it because I loved her. And, because I loved him.

Chapter 20

Sunday, July 7, 1996. London.

"I'm worried about you. We shouldn't have come." Rob stared across the table at Kate, who'd only picked at her food. She stared back.

"Stop worrying. I'm okay. We had to come, because if there is anything I can do, anything at all, to put Stanton away, I have to do it." She stabbed at a piece of chicken. "Fun and games are over for that...that monster."

Rob looked skeptical. "If you're not one hundred percent tomorrow, I don't want you taking the stand."

"Oh, I'm going to be one hundred percent. Two hundred percent." She forced a smile. "And yeah, I promise I'll rest."

The scene was surreal at Snaresbrook Crown Court the next day. Kate looked around the courtroom, wishing she could appreciate the fine woodwork, the classic styling.

Paulie, sitting to her right, leaned over. "It used to be an orphanage."

"I wish it still was," Rob muttered from Kate's left.

Kate rested her fingers across her belly, smoothing the navy blue maternity dress over the moderate swell. The Christmas baby was growing, sleeping, waiting to born in two months. A small commotion took her attention away, as the ushers escorted David Stanton to the defendant's dock.

Rob sighed, and Paulie stiffened. Kate's mouth went dry.

Stanton had pleaded not guilty, but Teasdale predicted it would be open and shut. Kate hoped so. She also desperately hoped her own trial would just go away. Not that there was any chance of that, however.

Opening arguments were made. Paulie was the first witness called. "Here we go," he whispered, then stood, straightened his tie. Sworn in, he sat down in the witness dock.

"Has he had his 'vitamins'?" Rob asked.

"Two. He couldn't do this otherwise," Kate whispered back, referring to the anti-anxiety medication Paulie had popped that morning.

The prosecutor paced, then approached.

"Mr. Bingham. Please limit your responses to my questions to the time period leading up to December 30, 1994 and to those events directly affecting the crime as accused. Now, if you will, describe your relationship with the defendant."

"We met here, in London, in 1981. We were introduced by a mutual friend, who thought David might fit in with our band. He later became the keyboardist. He left the band in 1983. We lost touch. We reconnected in 1991, and he joined the new band, but only briefly."

"On the night of December 30, 1994, you attended a holiday party at the home of Ian Flynn. Is this correct?"

"Yes, sir."

"Did you see the accused, Mr. David Stanton, at this party?"

"No, sir."

"When was the last time you saw Mr. Stanton?"

"It was at his home, in Los Angeles. January of 1992."

"And what was the occasion for you to be...with Mr. Stanton?"

Paulie drew a visible breath, kept his eyes focused ahead. "A social visit."

"Mr. Bingham, are you aware of Mr. Stanton's sexual preferences?"

"He's gay."

"And were you, at any time, partners in a homosexual relationship?"

"No. Absolutely not."

"But during this visit, in January of 1992, Mr. Stanton let it be known, did he not, that he wished to have such a relationship with you?"

Paulie looked down, wet his lips. Kate's own lips were moving, willing him to speak. Tell the truth, Paul. Say it.

"Yes. He did."

"And did you acquiesce? Were you interested in engaging Mr. Stanton?"

"No. I was not. We'd been friends a long time, and this was a complete surprise."

"And how did Mr. Stanton react to your rebuff, as it were?"

Kate expected an objection, but the defense table remained silent. She watched Paulie closely, wondering what and how much he would reveal. She caught his eye, and he fixed his gaze upon her.

"With physical abuse."

"Please elaborate."

"Objection." The defending barrister finally stood, and Kate exhaled.

The prosecutor was not to be dissuaded. "My Lord, the prosecution wishes to establish that Mr. Stanton's alleged fascination with Mr. Bingham has a direct bearing on this case. In fact, Mr. Bingham's refusal of Mr. Stanton's advances could be considered motivation...for retribution."

"Overruled."

"Please, Mr. Bingham. Proceed."

Paulie cleared his throat, turned slowly toward the defendant dock. Stanton's icy stare chilled Kate, made her stomach clench.

The prosecutor's voice softened only slightly. "I understand this is difficult. Would you say that Mr. Stanton became violent?"

"Yes."

"Would you also suggest that he used force, with regard to...actions and activities against your consent?"

Paulie turned he gaze back to the barrister and nodded.

"I'm sorry, Mr. Bingham. A verbal response is requested."

"Yes. Yes, sir. He...he assaulted me sexually."

Hot tears stinging her eyes, Kate groped for Rob's hand as a loud murmur washed through the courtroom.

"I see. And what was your response to this assault?"

"I fired him. I banished him from my life."

"You did not seek to press charges?"

"No."

"And why not?"

Paulie gave the prosecutor a sour smile. "Come now, an openly gay entertainer presses rape charges against another of the same? Do you honestly think credence would have been given, in the American justice system?" He shook his head. "No. Plus, I was married at the time. You must know, the press dogs my every move, and I didn't want to cause my family any more humiliation. It seemed better to just...forget."

"Were you concerned about retribution?"

"Clearly, not concerned enough."

"Thank you, Mr. Bingham."

Paulie was still quivering when he rejoined Kate and Rob. Neither man thought it prudent, but Kate took the stand when she was called. She was calm, sat straight and confident in the chair.

"I met him at the funeral of a friend of Paul's. I thought he was a nice guy, seemed to be a good friend to Paul. He started coming around to our house, visiting and doing little things to help us out after our daughter was born. He even came to the hospital."

"And did that routine eventually change?"

"Yes. He came to our house one day when Paulie was gone. He sat down and started trying to, to convince me to leave Paul. He said I was making Paul unhappy. He was trying to split us up."

"And was he successful?"

"No. Not at all."

"Did you know about the assault on your husband?"

"No. I did not."

"Why do you suppose Mr. Stanton was trying to split you up, as you say?"

"He wanted Paulie for himself." Kate shifted in the chair, turned to stare at Stanton. *You rat bastard. I hope you rot and die in prison for what you did to him. For what you did to Cheryl. And for what you did to me.*

"Thank you, Mrs. Evans."

When she returned to her seat, she blew out a breath. "They should reestablish capital punishment in this country just for him," she muttered.

The next witness called went by "Lee Jones," but Kate doubted that was his real name. This, apparently, was the protected witness that had come forth with information that broke the case.

"Please describe your actions on the night of 30 December, 1994."

"I know that chap," Paulie murmured.

"I tended bar at Ian Flynn's party."

"And as such, you saw a number of people come and go that evening."

"Yeah."

"Please, tell us what you recall."

"Well, there was a lot of blokes there. Ian told me to pour light. Some were doing various drugs, y'know. Lots of food, all around. I saw Paulie Bingham there. Chattin' up Jonny Beale. I was busy though. I didn't get a chance to pop over and say hello before they both left. So I asked m'mate, Billy, if he'd mind the booze for a bit so's I could catch up and pass on greetin's to Jon and Paulie."

"So you left the house and went outside, in hopes of catching Mr. Bingham before he got too far."

"Yeah. But by the time I got my coat and scarf on and managed to get out to the street, they were too far away. So I thought to smoke a fag before going back inside. I walked across the street, sat down on a little wall. It was dark. That's when I saw them."

"Saw whom, Mr. Jones?"

"This other chap. He comes out of nowhere and knocks. Ian comes out and they chat a bit, then both go back inside. The other bloke wasn't there long, he came back out and started walking away, following the same path as Paulie and Jon."

"Can you describe this second gentleman?"

"I didn't see his face much, except to say he was white, shorter than Ian, maybe five feet eight or nine. He was wearing a hoodie. A bit stout."

"What did you do next?"

"I waited a bit, finished the smoke, went back inside. Didn't think much about it until after poor Jonny turned up dead."

"Did you contact Mr. Flynn?"

"No. I didn't do anything at first. But after Paulie got off, I figured that the killer was still around, and that wasn't good. I got scared, so I called the police. I never did think Bingham did it, by the way."

Paulie flashed a brief smile and gave the young man a subtle nod.

The balance of the day was filled with repeat performances from forensics witnesses. Testimony of witnesses called in the previous trial was read to the jury. Finally, Kate, Rob and Paulie were ushered through throngs of paparazzi to a waiting car.

"You know they'll call Flynn tomorrow," Paulie said. The Chanticleer kitchen was cozy and warm, and Paulie withdrew a baking dish from the oven. "You will love this."

"Do you want help?" Kate said, getting up from the table.

"Ah ah ah. No. Sit. Rob, tie her down, will you?"

"Should we bring rotten tomatoes? Or would that be considered a weapon?" Rob asked.

"I think slingshots would be better," Kate said. "I despise that man. On many levels."

"With good reason, love." Paulie dipped a spoon into the corner of the casserole, tasted. "Mm. Okay. Let's devour. Milk?"

"Aren't we going to wait for Alec?"

"In a word, miss, no. Working late, as usual. Nuked leftovers for the good doctor."

Kate caught a look from Rob, and she shrugged behind Paulie's back.

The food was superb.

"Why didn't you cook like this when you were married to me?" she asked in mock irritation.

Paulie swallowed, took a gulp of milk. "Because I was never bored when I was married to you."

Rob rolled his eyes. "Methinks Mr. Bingham needs to get back behind a microphone."

"Good idea. Take me to the studio. Please. Now."

"You got it, pal. We should do a collaboration. All we need is an idea for a song. How about a little country tune like, 'Whose Wife Is She Today?' I have a catchy melody in mind."

"Cheek," Paulie scolded, but his face colored.

"I'm serious, dude. At least about getting you back out there. Unless you're planning to open a restaurant, I don't get that the chef's life is turning you on."

"I think it's a great idea. Come home with us. Come back to L.A," Kate agreed.

Paulie frowned at Kate. "You want me leave him?"

"No, I..." Kate felt the blood drain from her face. She hadn't meant that, had she? "I only meant, take a trip. Go into the studio with Rob. Wouldn't it be great? Surely Alec wouldn't mind. It's what you do. Or, what you did, before."

"Before I became a kitchen witch."

Tuesday, July 9, 1996.

Day two of the second Jon Beale murder trial commenced with Ian Flynn's walk to the witness box.

"Now, Mr. Flynn. I've reviewed the transcripts from the previous trial. You mentioned specifics of Mr. Bingham and Mr. Beale leaving the party. You did not mention yourself leaving, as attested to by Mr. Jones."

"I didn't leave the party, exactly."

"You did exit the premises, did you not?"

"Yes. I did." Ian Flynn's face hardened as he eyelids partially closed and he looked to his lap.

"Where did you go, sir, and for what purpose?"

"I merely stepped outside, to meet him."

"Him, sir?"

"Stanton. David Stanton."

"Would you identify the man you met outside?"

"Him. That's him." Flynn gestured briefly to the man sitting in the defendant's dock. "I invited him after he said he was a mate of Paulie's. He came in, sampled some wares, then asked after Paul. I told him Paulie was out with Jon, on their way to Paulie's house. He left then."

"I see. And when you heard that Mr. Beale had been murdered, were you not suspicious of Mr. Stanton?"

"Not particularly. After all, who am I to place blame? For all I knew, Paulie *had* killed dear Jon."

"But Mr. Bingham was acquitted. Did you still not wonder how Mr. Stanton might have been involved?"

"It crossed my mind. However, it's not my problem, now, is it? That would be Scotland Yard's problem, and yours."

His arrogance knows no bounds, Paulie thought, stewing in his seat. He leaned across Kate and whispered to Rob. "He copped a plea in exchange for his testimony."

Rob shook his head.

During the break for noonday meal, Paulie noticed the Beale family sitting in the same seats they occupied during his trial. If possible, they looked even more disheartened, more haggard than ever. He hated that they had to go through the ordeal again, relive all the horrible details.

Kate and Rob followed Paulie to where the Beales were just getting to the exit. Paulie stopped Mrs. Beale with a gentle hand to her elbow.

"Mrs. Beale, I want you to meet Kate, and her husband Rob. They wanted to say hello."

"Oh, so pleased to meet you."

Kate touched the older woman's arm. "I wish it was under better circumstances. I'm so sorry about...all this. Jon was...a nice young man," she managed, and Paulie knew it cost her. Rob, too, offered condolences. As they exited the courthouse, Paulie looked up to the dark clouds congregating over London. The defense would begin their case after lunch.

☞ **Rob and I almost had our first real argument over whether or not we should go to London for Stanton's trial. He, of course, my protective, semi-conservative husband, was reluctant to let me travel in my seventh month of pregnancy. Me, of course, bitch-on-wheels I could become when I wanted my way, insisted that my presence was crucial. I won, obviously.**

So it was that we'd barely returned from our incredibly wonderful Hawaiian honeymoon when I made our

travel plans to return to Britain. My doctor gave me the go-ahead, so Rob couldn't very well argue about my health. And he doesn't like to fight, in any case.

Our wedding was astonishingly perfect. We did add Kelly green into our scheme, and Paulie did escort me from the dressing room, down the sweeping country club staircase and then to the altar. We had a lark beforehand, getting ready in the bride's quarters with Cheryl, Bonny, Jo Jo and Shanie, and the Moms, of course. While I was fussing with his green satin cummerbund, Paul fastened a lovely set of pearls around my neck. At the top of the stairs, he insisted on taking off my shoes and carrying them for me until we reached the bottom, at which point he held my bouquet while I put my shoes back on. And when we reached that spot where we are supposed to stop, and the minister asked who gives this woman, he said, "I do," so loud and clear, then quickly leaned close and whispered, "never," before taking his seat beside our flower-girl daughter. But I didn't cry! That is, until I looked up and saw my patient, blindly devoted, excruciatingly handsome fiancé waiting with his hand out. At that point, I pretty much lost it.

I found out about the baby the day before the wedding, and of course I told only Rob. His delighted whoop thrilled me to the core. We told everyone else when we returned from Maui. No one was more excited than Gramma Evans.

I don't recall talking to Paulie very much in the months between that day and our arrival at Heathrow, where he picked us up himself. We'd seen Alec only once, and while exceedingly cordial, he was distant and disengaged. Paulie said he was working with a particularly difficult patient at the moment.

Paul's not seeing Megan anymore. At least not in the manner he was before. He didn't tell me, but as usual, the Paulie-Kate connection dumped the info right into my head. I'm glad, and yet, I worry about his obvious loneliness.

– Mrs. Kate Evans

Chapter 21

Wednesday, July 10, 1996

Stanton's barrister called Paul Bingham to the witness box. Paulie was edgy, waiting, always waiting, for the drugs to kick in.

"Now. At this point, in 1992, when you say you last saw the defendant, you had not yet made the acquaintance of the victim, Jon Beale. Is that correct?"

"Yes. I didn't meet Jon until...1994."

"So you could not possibly have told Mr. Stanton about your friendship with Mr. Beale."

"No, sir."

"Let's return to your testimony concerning January, 1992, when you accompanied my client to his home in Malibu, California. This was not the first night you had spent with the defendant, socially, as you called it."

"I didn't spend the night there by own my own free will."

"But you went out with Mr. Stanton that evening of your own free will, and on several other occasions during the weeks preceding the night in question. Correct?"

"No."

"You are denying that you accompanied Mr. Stanton on several nights to various gay bars in the Los Angeles area, where you imbibed alcoholic drinks and watched entertainment together?"

"I went with him a few times. I wouldn't say several. It was nothing out of the ordinary. Nothing unusual between friends."

"During which time you ignored obvious indications of Mr. Stanton's growing affection for you?"

"Affection? Affection? That's the most preposterous label for that kind of sickness I've ever heard."

"Objection. This line of questioning is preposterous!" The prosecutor swept his arm through the air, anger reddening his face. "How can Mr. Bingham's personal reaction to the defendant have any bearing of this...this question of murder?"

The judge tilted his head, sighed. "Overruled. The Court wishes to hear this out. Continue, Counselor."

"Let me rephrase the question, Mr. Bingham. Do you deny that you led Mr. Stanton to believe that his romantic advances were not only acceptable, but desired? And that, perhaps, what you experienced was not an assault at all?"

Paulie jumped to his feet, pointed his finger at David Stanton. "I not only deny it, but your words disgust me. That man, that man there is a sick, perverted bastard and not worth the steam off my piss!"

The judge pounded his hammer and the courtroom security officers rushed forward. The defense barrister held up his hands. "It's all right. Mr. Bingham, please, sit down. Is it possible, that perhaps events occurring subsequent to the nights of January, 1992, have, shall we say, muddied the memories of those evenings? Evenings when you allowed, without protest, Mr. Stanton to kiss you?"

Chest heaving, Paulie did not sit down, but stood staring at the attorney. "No, sir. My memories of those evenings are crystal clear. And once Mr. Stanton made his intentions clear, I made mine clear."

The barrister abruptly turned. "No further questions."

"Are you all right?" Kate asked, when Paulie rejoined her and Rob.

"No. I'm a fucking flaming wreck. I need to get out of here."

"It's only around forty minutes until the break. Can you make it that long?"

"I suppose."

He couldn't feel anything, didn't know how his legs would carry him. As Kate headed for the restroom, Rob directed Paulie to the greens outside the courthouse.

"She'll find us," Rob murmured. "She has a built-in homing device."

Outside, Paulie glared across the expanse of verdant grasses at the massive collection of photographers camped out, tripods set, telephoto lenses trained.

"Look at those scumbags."

"Smile, Paul."

Paulie turned his back on them, moved closer to Rob. "Are you holding?"

"Holding what? Are you crazy?"

"Look. I just asked."

"Yeah, like I would first be able to get anything past my drug-sniffing wife, then waltz right into Britain's Crown Court with a pocketful of weed." Rob laughed. "Oh. But that's me. Not you."

"Clearly. Let's not forget that you're you and I'm me. It can get confusing. Although it's rather fun to see her rattled. How long before she's back?"

"Judging from the line at the ladies' head, I'd say... three to five minutes."

"Good." Paulie pulled a cigarette and a book of matches from his pocket. "I bummed this on the way in. Better than nothing."

"She'll see it in the papers," Rob warned, tilting his head to the media hounds.

"Fuck them."

Rob shoved his hands into his pockets, paced as Paulie smoked. "You know, I think Kat's right. You should come back with us when this little shindig is over. I got to thinking about that collaboration. Besides being fun, it could be very lucrative."

"I'm all for making money. But right now, I have bigger issues to deal with."

"Such as? Something more than this fiasco?"

"My husband doesn't understand me."

Rob chuckled. "Not sure how to respond to that."

"Don't bother. I'm actually quite surprised he didn't cancel everything to come along and keep tabs on me."

"Keep tabs? As in, the jealous spouse routine?"

Paulie nodded, took one last drag on the cigarette and tossed it into the grass. "Did you see the cameras at Chanticleer? Said it was for security. But he's watching me. They record my comings and goings. He calls me several times a day. Megs helped me get a second cell, so that I can call round without worry."

"Jesus. I had no idea."

"He's good at the front. Don't get the wrong idea, mate. I think the world of Alec. He's a good man. Honest, loving, sexy, if you will. He sees to it that I want for nothing, except, perhaps, a little trust."

"Button down. Your wife is coming."

"My wife? Now you're trying to confuse me again, sweetheart." Paulie turned to watch Kate as she walked toward them across the grass. Sunlight was spotty, and he marveled as she came in and out of the beams that poked through the otherwise cloudy London sky, stepping carefully to avoid pitfalls. Her dark blue frock fluttered over her knees, the little bulge showing occasionally as the dress swayed, invoking memories of another time, another baby. She smiled, and he didn't bother to care whether it was Rob, or himself, who inspired her joy.

"Whew. What are you guys doing way out here?"

"Walking off anxiety," Rob explained, bending for a quick kiss. "You okay?"

"There was a line. A few girls let me go ahead because of this," she said, pointing to her belly. "But while I was waiting, I was thinking up ways to take care of this trial quickly."

"Did they involve machetes and guns?" Paulie muttered.

"Worse. You don't want to know what I would do to him if I could. It would shock even you." Kate reached up and touched Paulie's face. "You feeling any better?"

"Not really. Not as bad, I guess. Ev here has a calming effect. Thanks for bringing him along, darling."

☞ *I was long to remember that afternoon, that vision of her walking toward us. In my memory, it was all in slo-mo, like the boy and girl in that TV commercial who are running across the field of wildflowers toward each other, twinkles in their lovelorn eyes. My eyes were still lovelorn, too. Or forlorn, whatever your pleasure.*

Ev's innuendo was not lost on me. She belonged to both of us, still. It didn't matter to me, anymore, that she slept with him, made her home with him, carried his child. It wasn't like I hadn't done all that already. In return for his generosity, I tied off all the strings I used to pull with her. We had, perhaps, finally settled into something that worked for all of us. I also finally understood that she would never abandon me. That realisation helped me to let her love him, to keep the jealousy at bay.

I'd given up on trying to explain it to Alec. I couldn't really blame him, because there were no precedents for a relationship like mine and Kate's. Nothing to call upon, compare to. He was entitled to his discomfort, and I tried to minimalise it all. He was, otherwise, extremely good to me, and I was trying hard to make it work.

Ev has become the brother I never had. He's far smarter and a helluva lot more centered than I will ever be. He is the best gift I could ever give Kate, and I think that says enough. And short of a divorce, I plan to take him up on his offer. Perhaps a duet of 'Leather and Lace'? –Paulie, spinning again

The trial resumed. Kate had grown lethargic over the break, but became rapt when word went around that David Stanton would take the stand in his own defense. She was humming inside, and it wasn't a song; just a low vibration, not unlike an adrenaline rush, that amped up her heartbeat, made her palms sweat.

She mentally called upon her foulest words as Stanton was sworn in. Memories of his hands on her skin could no longer be ignored, the icy touch of the shears he'd used to cut the clothing from her body. Cheryl's excited face when talking about him, how nice he was, how he might be 'the one'. And Paulie's suffering, the pained mortification at the unspeakable acts the deviant had imposed on him.

The defense barrister began direct examination, getting past the preliminaries recounting how the defendant had met

Paulie Bingham, how he had, in fact, grown fond of Paulie during their time together with the Bingham Boys. His aim seemed to be proving that Stanton had followed Paulie with the intention of reconciling, not murdering a potential rival.

"When I saw him again, at Pritchard's funeral, I realized just how much I'd missed having him around. I knew that if I could just earn his trust and respect, I could convince him to pursue a more intimate relationship."

"And what did you do, to earn that trust?"

"Nothing any friend wouldn't do."

"Just what happened next?"

"Paulie had confided in me that his then-wife, Katrina, was disdainful of his homosexuality. It pained me to see him denying himself the pleasure he once valued so much. I thought it in his best interest to gently sway him away from such hetero nonsense. Hence my invitations to go clubbing. When his wife got wind of our dates, she unsurprisingly abandoned him."

Kate forced herself to stay calm when she realized she was grinding her teeth. Paulie, however, looked about ready to come out of his chair. She reached for his hand, found it clammy. He let her hold it for a moment, then pulled away, distracted.

"You say Mrs. Bingham abandoned her husband. How so?"

"She took their daughter and went to live in another state, with her parents."

"I see. And how did Mr. Bingham react?"

"He was upset, of course, for a bit. But he ultimately understood that what he was trying to do, that is, live a lie as a straight man, was a fantasy. That's when I brought him to my home in Malibu, California."

The barrister walked away, as if weighing his options. Kate hoped her eyes were burning a hole in the back of his suit jacket. When he returned to the defendant, he did, indeed, change his angle.

"Mr. Stanton, how would you characterize Mr. Bingham with regard to his clarity of mind?"

"Definitely confused. So much so that he gets things mixed up. Likely due to his parents' lack of support for his sexual persuasion, and his heavy drug use in the early 80's."

"Objection! This line of questioning, and speculation about the witness is irrelevant and possibly misleading. Mr. Bingham is not on trial here."

"Sustained. Barrister Teague, please amend your direction."

"My Lord, the defense wishes to establish that witness Paul Bingham may have, indeed, inadvertently misled the court, due to his propensity for poor recollection of events in his past."

"The objection is sustained. Opinion and speculation have no bearing. The jury will disregard statements concerning Mr. Bingham's...clarity of mind."

Rob tilted his head. "This is going to get worse before it gets better."

Teague continued to question Stanton about events leading up to the murder, consistently pointing to Paulie's alleged secret crush on the defendant.

"I did not, in fact, already know Mr. Flynn. He and Paulie were mates back when the Boys were founded, but I don't recall meeting him."

"So how did you happen by his house on the evening of Mr. Flynn's party?"

"Paulie invited me, of course. Although I doubt he'll admit it. I received a call from him that afternoon, he was in a payphone kiosk near Leicester Square, or so he said."

Paulie abruptly stood. "That's a lie!"

"See? I knew he'd deny it. Nonetheless, he left before I arrived. According to Flynn, Paulie didn't want squat to do with Beale, but the bloke would not refrain from harassment. It was my original intention to stop them, and to scare Beale off."

Kate persuaded Paulie to sit down. Heated, he obliged, but his hands were clenched in rage.

"Did you encounter Mr. Beale then, and accomplish your goal?"

Stanton sighed, looked away. "No. I had a change of heart. I decided I should see Paulie under better circumstances at a later time."

"What did you do next?"

"I left then. Went back to my hotel room."

"At what time, would you say, you arrived at your hotel room?"

"9:55 p.m. The bartender in the lobby served me a drink, and I went to bed."

"Liar," Paulie grumbled. "Lying asshole wanker."

Kate placed her hand on his thigh. "Absolutely. Just wait until the prosecutor gets his hook into him."

"Cross examination, M'Lord?"

"Proceed."

"Mr. Stanton. Let's return to your visit to Mr. Flynn's house. When you discovered that Mr. Bingham had left the premises, what did you do?"

"I took a sip off a tankard of ale and, as Flynn mentioned, I tasted a few crisps and such."

"You must have been quite hungry after your long journey."

"Sorry?"

"Oh, you know, your flight from Los Angeles that afternoon. You flew coach, is that correct?"

Stanton shot a look at Teague. The Prosecuting Barrister Hunt paced quietly for a few moments while the defense team shuffled papers.

"In fact, you were in seat 34A of United Airlines Flight 456 for the hours surrounding the time period known as afternoon, when you received your alleged phone call from Mr. Bingham. Arriving at Mr. Flynn's residence when you did, waiting alongside his front garden in the cold shrubbery couldn't have allowed for much time to eat. But of course, that's irrelevant. Perhaps your memory is a little cloudy. So let's move on. You said you considered "scaring" Mr. Beale off. How did you intend to do that?"

Flustered, Stanton swallowed, wet his lips. "Didn't really think about it. I was going to tell him off, I suppose. Explain that Paulie...Paulie already had a lover."

"You."

"I doesn't matter who. The point was—"

"The point was, you never intended to tell anyone 'off'. Your goal was much more drastic, wasn't it? To make certain that

Mr. Beale would not, let me rephrase that, could never attempt to seduce Mr. Bingham again."

"I didn't kill Jon Beale!"

"Who did, then? Who do you think laid in wait for this young, heartsick boy, alone in the fog on the Heath? Wasn't it another heartsick man, a man suffering from years of unrequited love, a man so needy and so angry that he'd rather send the object of his affection to prison for life than see him with another?"

"That's utterly ridiculous. I didn't even know Beale, and if you're truly looking for his killer, you'll look no farther than this very courtroom. Paul Bingham himself had motive and opportunity."

"And yet, you are aware that Mr. Bingham was tried for the crime, and found not guilty."

"So I've heard. Could've been Flynn, as well. There's no love lost there, between him and Paulie. He could have easily set Paul up. It was his knife, after all."

"Actually, Mr. Stanton, Mr. Flynn has a substantial alibi, having been back inside his home, entertaining a number of guests. The bartender at your hotel left early, at 9:30 p.m. on 30 December, as there were no patrons. No, it seems that the only one without a solid accounting of their whereabouts that night is you."

Stanton looked down his nose. "That is, if you believe Paulie was actually with Dr. Doyle."

Whispers circulated.

"Are you suggesting, sir, that Mr. Bingham does not have a credible alibi?"

"I'm suggesting that neither Paulie nor his snooty, highbrowed lover have credible alibis."

The commotion grew in the courthouse. Paulie touched his forehead, blinked his eyes.

The judge leaned toward his microphone. "Unless he can substantiate his claims, the defendant will refrain from further speculation."

"Think about it," Stanton continued, animated. "There's no one but the two, who claimed to be together. Lovers defending one another, wouldn't you say? Doyle's nothing more than a miscreant himself, you know. He'd have put that knife into Beale's neck, if he wasn't such a pale faced pansy."

Rob rubbed at his chin. "He knows Alec. The plot thickens."

The prosecutor stood directly in front of Stanton. "Try as you might to discredit others, the fact remains, Mr. Stanton, that you harbor unrequited love. That you plotted, all along, to kill Mr. Beale and frame Mr. Bingham, in retribution for Mr. Bingham's rejection of your affection—as further evidenced by your loathing for his current, common law partner. You never planned to 'scare off' young Beale. What you did plan was to brutally murder an innocent man, a man whose only crime was to take a liking to someone you coveted and could not have. And because you couldn't have Mr. Bingham, you were resigned that no one could have him after he was sentenced to life in prison for a murder he did not commit."

Kate could see Stanton growing more agitated as the barrister needled him. She hadn't expected the prosecutor to go for the kill so soon.

"You worked with Mr. Flynn. Knew Mr. Beale and Mr. Bingham would both be attending the party. Mr. Flynn did his part, created a scenario for the two in which they would, most likely, leave simultaneously. He knowingly or unknowingly provided the implicating weapon. All that was left was for you to wait for Mr. Beale to be alone on the Heath, where you accosted him, forced him to his knees and stabbed him mercilessly." The prosecutor held up his notes as if they were pages of evidence. "Do yourself a favor, Mr. Stanton. Own up to your grievous crime, and ask your maker for forgiveness!"

Stanton grew still, his fingers curled around the arms of his chair. The courtroom went eerily silent.

He's going to confess! Kate held her breath, clasped her hands in her lap.

Teague got to his feet and started to approach Stanton, who dismissed him with a wave. The defendant narrowed his eyes, stared back at the prosecutor. "All right then. All right. But if I'm going down, then I'm taking him down with me. Because this wasn't my idea, you see. No. I did not fly all the way from Los Angeles to do this on my own. I was paid, good money, to take care of this little problem. Maybe he wasn't there, maybe he didn't wield the knife, but he was there in spirit. It was his hand as much as mine who ended Jon Beale's life."

After a round of gasps, the courtroom quieted again as the shocked prosecutor lowered his papers, directed two last questions to David Stanton.

"About whom are you speaking, sir? Who paid you to kill Jon Beale?"

"Isn't it obvious? Why, the upstanding and prominent doctor! Who couldn't be bothered to sit in with his poor, beleaguered partner during this dark hour. Alec Doyle's the one who contacted me, asked me to come, paid my airfare. Suggested I make certain that Mr. Beale didn't move in on Paulie a second time and ruin the good doc's chances with the everlasting boy pop star!"

"Oh my God!" Kate exclaimed.

Paulie clamped a hand over his mouth and shrank back against his seat..

"And not only that," Stanton shouted, over the din of the court's reaction to his accusation, "Doyle was the one who came up with the idea of quieting, for good, the slutty little ex who couldn't seem to keep her snatch away from Paulie's cock!"

The hammer pounded, had little effect on the chaos that engulfed the courtroom. Kate could barely get a breath as people around her shouted their shock and disgust. Someone was screaming, and Rob was trying to say something, trying to take her arm. In slow motion, she turned from left to right, realizing at last the one screaming was Paulie.

"Paul!" she shrieked, throwing her arms around him as he collapsed and pulled her onto the floor with him. "Paul, oh, Paulie, it's all right, it's all right..."

His unseeing eyes were open, fearful. He was muttering, and Kate lowered her ear to his lips. "He didn't do it, Mum. He didn't do it, Mum," he repeated in a desperate whisper. She managed to get his head into her lap, and he instinctively curled his body around her. Rob, too, was behind her on the floor, yelling at people to move away and would somebody please get a goddam doctor?

"It's okay, Paul. It's okay. Shh." She rocked him, ignoring the policemen who were now pressing around her.

"Where is Dr. Doyle, Mr. Bingham? We need to pick him up."

Kate looked up, snarled. "Can't you see he's not well? He can't tell you anything right now."

Rob held up his hand. "Please. Give us some room. Dr. Doyle has an office in Kensington. It shouldn't be too hard to find him. I'm sure you have the home address in Hampstead."

The sights and sounds around her dimmed away, as Kate focused all of her attention on Paulie. She held him close, rocking, whispering, kissing his forehead. His words made no sense, but he clung to her, wouldn't let go when the paramedics arrived. Kate, too, was reluctant to let them pull him from her arms.

It wasn't until the ambulance rolled away that her consciousness fully returned, and she let Rob hold her while she cried.

☙ **Why do things happen like they do? Is it all part of some grand scheme? Some pre-booked flight on the ride of life, complete with all the joys and tragedies already written?**

Alec Doyle's story was surprisingly like Stanton's-- only in reverse. The doctor asserted that Stanton had contacted him, with information he'd hacked about Paulie and me, and an offer to scare off young Jon before Alec suffered the same fate I had. Alec had, he claimed, naively bought into the plot, advancing Stanton airfare and money for lodging. He owned up to the jealousy, the acute fear that he would lose Paulie again. I had to admit I identified with that. But he swore he never thought it would come to murder.

As to his part in my ordeal, Alec also swore he had nothing to do with the crime. He may have, he admitted, unwittingly given Stanton details about me, the baby, and Jon Beale he wouldn't ordinarily have known, details Stanton eventually and anonymously fed to Mindon's team during Paulie's trial. Do I believe him? Rob does. But I'm not so quick to decide. Another trial is forthcoming. Because Stanton's confession included his involvement in my

abduction, we are hoping he will just enter a guilty plea and forego the trial here.

My beloved Paulie is living in a country rest home in Scotland, not far from the Queen's summer lodgings in Aberdeenshire. Balmoral Castle is only a stone's throw, I understand. His recovery from the breakdown is painstakingly slow. He has a personal attendant, a young man named Jeffrey, who keeps me informed of Paul's progress and state of mind. He reads my letters aloud, shows Paulie the photos of Bonny I send every week or so. There is, of course, a telephone, but Paulie is still reluctant to talk on it.

Our baby is due any day, and Rob and I have never been closer. We are comfortable with Paulie's care, so we're able to focus on our own joys of the moment. As soon as I am able to travel again, we will be winging our way to Scotland, children in tow. Hopefully by Christmas.

What happens next? In my more perfect world, Paulie will come back to California with us, and make that record with Rob.

Stanton will hang himself in Pentonville Prison.

Alec will repent for his part, get serious therapy, and stay away from Paulie. Maybe he should do some time, if the jury finds him guilty of collusion.

Rob and I will have more babies, but I will stay slender and sexy. Ha!

And Paulie will find love. Someone who neither over-covets nor abuses him. Someone with whom he can be his blessedly beautiful self, without fear of loss or suffocation.

I can be an idealist if I want.

—Katrina Newman Bingham Evans

Chapter 22

December, 1996. Los Angeles, CA

Luca Paul Evans signaled his readiness to be born on September 25th, exactly nine months after his Christmas morning conception. Although she felt better prepared, Kate was surprised to learn that her baby could take the more convention route this time; her doctor determined that the Caesarian section she dreaded would not be necessary. So another new experience lay in store as Rob helped her through the withholding and the pushing.

At two and a half months, Luc was deemed ready to travel, and Kate hurriedly bought seats to Edinburgh. After a day of recovery and a little shopping, they rented a van and Rob braved the wrong-way drivers on the northern route to chilly Aberdeenshire.

The 'home' was a large cottage, set amidst a stand of trees, bordering a normally grassy meadow. Today, it was sunny and crispy cold, the remnants of the last snow still in evidence. Kate tucked Luca into a front loading baby pack and Bonny into a warm woolen Scottish plaid coat.

Jeffrey was waiting for them at the door.

"So nice to meet you in person," he said. "Please, hurry in to our warm parlour."

Kate sized up the young man, whom she deemed to be between twenty-five and thirty and decidedly queer. Three other residents relaxed in the room, but Jeffrey motioned toward the back of the house. "Paulie's out in the sun porch."

"Does he know we're here?"

"I told him you were coming today. He's looking forward to your visit."

Rob took Bonny's hand. "Remember how we decided that we were going to let Mommy go see Daddy first?"

"Yup. I remember."

"Okay, then."

Jeffrey grinned. "You are far more beautiful than your pictures, Miss Bonny." He squatted down. "Do you know, your daddy speaks fondly of you every single day?"

Bonny giggled, clung to Rob's hand.

"Out that side door, and down the hillside only a bit, there is a partly frozen pond that's quite nice to visit." Jeffrey gestured. "And Kate, if you'll follow me."

"Okay. Let's go, Daddy Rob," Bonny said, tugging. "Mummy will come tell us when she's through with Daddy."

Paulie was alone, standing with his back to her, peering out the large picture window off the back of the sun porch. Kate felt a flutter in her stomach at the sight of him. She moved close, coyly snaked her hand into his. He didn't move, other than to squeeze her hand in response.

"Don't be rude, darling. I've brought a guest."

He turned then, looked first into her face, then down at the roundish, blue corduroy pack strapped across her chest. Kate unlaced the top, peeled down the sides to reveal the sleeping baby's soft, downy covered head.

"This is Luca. But I'm afraid he's the one being rude, now."

Paulie reached in, touched the baby's cheek with the back of a finger.

"Such beauty could make one cry."

Kate smiled up at him, the sound of his voice filling her with gladness. "He's a good baby."

"All babies are good, aren't they? Have a sit?"

"I think so. Yeah, I'd like to sit."

"You've come an awfully long way." He spoke slowly, carefully choosing his words.

"The moon is a long way." She took his hand, again, held it between both of hers. "I have never missed you so much as I have these past months. I've been waiting for this day for weeks."

"I'm sorry I couldn't talk to you."

"It's okay. Jeffrey's kept me up to date."

"Jeffrey." Paulie nodded. "A godsend."

"Good. I'm thankful that you have someone to care for you. He says..." Kate paused, hoping she wasn't saying the wrong thing. "He says you may be ready to come home soon."

Paulie smiled, but for all its sweetness, it was also sad. "I have no home to come to."

She knew what he meant. He'd never return to Hampstead. And Peg now cohabitated with her constable. Kate could see how it must look to Paulie.

"Home is where you make it. Let me show you something. Get up."

Paulie stood, offered his hand, helped her get to her feet with the baby. She walked him to the bank of side windows across the room, pointed outside. "Look at that. Do you see? Do you see two pieces of your family out there? As long as you have family, you'll always have a home."

He stared, his eyes trained on Bonny as she ran through the meadow, new coat trailing behind her like a cape, her long auburn curls shimmering. Rob, nearby, leaned against a tree watching. Paulie's smile was warm, refreshing, honest.

"What does she know?"

"That you've been working, hard, in a place that has no telephones. Secret mission stuff. She's a worrier, so I couldn't begin to say anything about any kind of illness. She's imaginative."

He nodded. "Should I see her?"

"Of course you should. When you're ready."

Kate could feel Luca squirming, and she reopened the pack. She sat back down on the couch, gently lifted the baby out.

"Here. Hold your godson."

"My—my godson? Are you joking?"

Kate grinned. "Come on. You know how to do this."

Before he could protest, Kate placed the infant in his arms.

"What if I—"

"Shh. You won't."

The baby eyed him, reached up and tried to grasp Paulie's chin. "Look at that. Clever little bugger. He has your eyes, darling."

Her heart swelled. She watched as Paulie admired the baby for a full two minutes.

"What's this godson nonsense, anyway?"

Kate shrugged. "He's yours. You are second in command, if anything ever happens, you know, to us."

"Truly."

"Yup."

"Hmm."

"So are you up to seeing your daughter?" Kate asked, taking Luca back and laying him down on the baby blanket she'd placed on the couch between them.

"I want to."

"But?"

"But...no buts. Just...give me a few more minutes."

"Okay. She's waited this long, a few more minutes won't hurt."

"How is she adjusting?"

"To what? The baby?"

"Yeah. To everything."

"Beautifully. I'm careful to, you know, give her lots of attention. But she's got so much confidence, she really adapts well."

"She surely didn't get that confidence from me."

"No, maybe not. But she has your good heart. And your beautiful eyes."

Paulie looked away, but Kate took a chance and touched his cheek, gently turning him back toward her.

"Would it be too much to ask for a little love, for your soul mate?"

Paulie drew in a deep breath, sighed.

"I'm not the same person anymore. My kisses won't mean the same."

Kate took a moment, looked down at the baby, then back at Paulie. "I don't want to upset you, or disappoint you in any way. I know you've been through a lot. But that is just about the biggest load of crap I've ever heard come from your lips."

He looked surprised, at first, then reached a tentative hand to her shoulder, slipping it beneath her hair and around the back of her neck. He licked his lips, a brief smile flashing.

"Crap, eh?" he murmured, then moved slowly closer until the tip of his nose touched hers. She could feel his breath, the warmth of his skin. She didn't move.

At last he moved forward, pressing his lips against hers. The kiss was affectionate, pure. He held her there, lips to lips, for just a moment, whispered softly.

"I should know better than to talk crap to you, Kate."

☞ *I wasn't being maudlin when I said I was a different person. I was, in some ways, altered forever by the events of 1994, 95 and 96. But I was soon to find out that one thing had not changed at all. It wasn't even the kiss. It was just the way she spoke to me.*

It took me a long while to accept what had happened. My care was first rate. One of the women there took me to chapel, reminded me that forgiveness was divine and she knew I wanted that divine-ness for myself. I worked hard, there were so many people to forgive.

Ev and I cut five tracks together in 1997. I had more fun writing and recording those songs than anything else I'd ever done. We put together an album, the balance of the tunes divided between us. The media had fun, too, wagging their tongues about Kate's husbands singing of their woebegone times together. We laughed, all the way to the effing bank. (And yes, I've had to clean up my mouth some, due to my mynah bird daughter.)

Jeffrey came back to L.A. with me, and we have an imperfect, but loving, relationship. He is six years my junior, but wise beyond my years. He and Kate get along wonderfully, all I could ask for. They are, surprisingly (or not) a lot alike. Jeffrey just may be "the one"!

On New Year's Day, 1998, Kate announced she was, once again, sprogged up, and Cheryl smugly flashed a two caret rock on her left hand. Not long after, Alec granted me a theoretical divorce from inside prison, and when he was released in May, he came to see me at my townhouse in Westlake Village. He came, he said, to apologise, and to wish me well. I felt sorry for the bloke, and I made him a cup of tea.

June was interesting. David Stanton died in Pentonville Prison, of an apparent suicide. Word from U.K.'s gay underbelly, however, says he was offed by a couple of homophobic cons. Kate was particularly upset by the whole incident. I'm not sure why, except that she (like me) probably felt a bit unsettled for wishing him dead.

We live close to Ev and Kate, and this makes it easy to share Bonny's love. There was a tough moment when she went back to school after summer break, and a classmate asked if her father was a faggot. I wanted to laugh and cry at the same time. I called Kate in a panic, and she and Ev came round to help me and Jeff sort it all out with her. It was a day I knew would come, a day I hoped we'd be prepared for. She went back to school filled with self-righteous indignation and a seven-year-old head full of admonitions about tolerance. I was encouraged when she did not return home with a black eye.

Tolerance is an everyday word in our home, as is communication, trust and benevolence. If I've learned anything over the past fifteen years, it's that I cannot live without these things. Why I ever tried I'll just have to chalk up to ignorance and innocence.

Last month, Kate called me, calmly asked if I could pop round and give her a lift to Los Robles. I said sure, what's that, and she said "it's a hospital, numb nuts." Rob was out of town for the day, and, well, her next child was ready to drop. We had a few minutes, between her verbal assaults, to chat while waiting for her second son to be born. I was much better this time round, and she kindly refrained from smacking me. Ev arrived when all the hard work was over, but I didn't mind. We three held hands and laughed until we cried. Kate was right. Family is home, and they are my home.

At thirty-seven, I can finally look in the mirror and see myself, recognise and feel decent inside my own skin. I finally got what it was all about. It was about Paul Philip Bingham coming out from behind all the masks and getting real.

Thank you, darling. ♥ Paulie

❧◦❧

The author hopes you've enjoyed Paulie and Kate's story, and if so, that you will share your thoughts with others. Thank you!

Beacon Street Books

http://BeaconStreetBooks.com

Meet Anne Carter

Creating fiction gives one the power to design other lives, filled with romance and adventure, intrigue and passion. My own writing career began in middle school creative writing class, inspiring me to later major in literature. All it took was one teacher' encouragement and I was on my way.

I'm the author of seven published novels, including mystery, romance, paranormal, alternative romance and even a middle grade reader. As for the personal stuff, I'm a Virgo, a procrastinator, like warm better than cold and drink neither Coke nor Pepsi. I was born in the Midwest but migrated to California as a child. My hobbies include doll collecting, photo restoration and writing, of course. My favorite sport is ice hockey, my favorite TV shows include Elementary, Person of Interest, NCIS, Downton Abbey, LOST, Flash Forward and Gray's Anatomy. I am married to my hero of 30+ years and have 3 great kids.

As a free-lance writer, I hang out at my website, Facebook, and other fun cyber spots..

Visit me at http://www.anne-carter.com

Also by Anne Carter:

UNMASKING PAULIE BINGHAM
(BOOK I OF PAULIE & KATE SERIES)

STARCROSSED ROMANCES:

STARCROSSED HEARTS
A HERO'S PROMISE
THE GYSPY IN ME (FALL, 2014)

BEACON POINT ROMANCES:

EVER & ALWAYS (PREQUEL)
POINT SURRENDER
CAPE SEDUCTION
ANGEL'S GATE

ALTERNATIVE ROMANCE NOVELLA:

STARFIRE